A DELICATE AFFAIR

DECADES: A JOURNEY OF AFRICAN AMERICAN
ROMANCE

LINDSAY EVANS

RED HILLS PUBLISHING

DEAR READER

Dear Reader,

A Delicate Affair is the first book in the *Decades: A Journey of African American Romance* series. This historical series consists of twelve books, each set in one of twelve decades between 1900 and 2010. Each story focuses on the romance between African American protagonists, but also embraces the African American experience within that decade.

I'm so proud to be a part of this unique series and so excited to launch it with my story, which is set in the 1900s. I hope that through reading A Delicate Affair, you'll become as enthralled with this decade as I am.

To find out more about the authors and the stories involved in the Decades series, please like our Facebook page, https://www.facebook.com/decades2018.

Thank you for reading,
Lindsay

A DELICATE AFFAIR

1

Golden knew he was in trouble when she walked in.

Brown skin, thick hair, a lioness of a woman striding with a pride of other beauties wearing expensive dresses. They were obviously rich. Young. At least, younger than the crowd that usually ended up at Rosie's juke joint. Younger than Golden's twenty-six. More than half the men in the crowded, smoky dance bar turned to watch the three of them, but he only saw her.

Clive, a guy Golden trusted and who was the reason he had the luck of playing at Rosie's in the first place, jerked his head up from the piano and tilted his head at Golden. The sign for, "What's going on?"

Damn. Ten years, on-and-off, of being friends with Golden apparently gave Clive a clue when Golden's attention veered away from where it should have been.

Golden tipped his head toward the door. Clive, not missing a single key on the piano he played like a madman, looked over at the girls. No way would his friend know which one had made Golden just about swallow his tongue.

"No chance." His friend merely mouthed the words, rolled his eyes, and gave his full attention to the ragtime he pounded out of the piano, placed sideways so Clive could see the audience and rile them up when he stood, shaking out one long leg and then the other, dancing while he played. The music-hungry Saturday night crowd ate it up.

In front of the stage, the sunken dance floor was packed body-to-body. People danced and gyrated and generally had a good-old time while the music played. Marley, the only woman in their band of four, belted out songs about heartbreak and lust while Winston, quiet and quietly intense, tormented the crowd with a rhythm from his pair of tall African drums.

Even though the place was crammed packed to the rafters, Big Ed, the galoot by the front door, hustled over to take care of the giggling girls. He waved them toward a table near the front of the stage and off the side from the dancers. Damn near within touching distance, if Golden got bold enough. He plucked at the strings of his banjo, improvising around Clive's loud and lively rag.

Golden's fingers were sore from playing all night, but he was having too much fun to care. The crowd was jumping and that girl was hot as the fire in his mama's kitchen.

Watching her, he didn't so much as twitch the wrong way. He couldn't mess up the music. Only he—and Clive—knew he was sweating like a hog at the butcher with that fine girl breezing between tables to sit at the big one up front.

Golden knew Rosie, the owner of the juke joint and a notoriously ornery woman, had been saving the main table for her man. But as soon as the girls gestured toward the table with their perfumed and pampered fingers, Rosie gave it up easier than a whore on Saturday night. Those rich girls meant money in her pocket.

Golden had only been in Washington, D.C. for about seven months, but he had already seen what money and power could buy. The only difference up here was that the money and influence was thrown around by Negroes, and people jumped up mighty quick to do whatever these rich Negroes wanted.

The band's latest song wound down to almost nothing and, suddenly, Golden felt everything he'd been too lost in the music to notice before. The sweat running down his face. The rough chafing of the new suit at his wrists every time he moved his hands along the banjo. The hunger that cramped his belly from not eating since his morning shift at Joe's, the restaurant where he worked most days.

Anyone not dancing clapped and jumped to their feet while the rich girls spread themselves around the table, chattering with each other and looking around like they were at a zoo or something. With their bright clothes and brighter laughter, they were like the gems scattered in his mama's jewelry box.

One girl wore red, another green. But the one he couldn't keep his eyes off wore white. Bits of the dress sparkled, and she seemed like a diamond among the others. Expensive and untouchable, cool despite her loud and frequent laughter.

From the way they leaned toward Big Ed and stopped him from walking off, Golden could tell they were demanding drinks. But Big Ed shook his head and gestured back toward the kitchen, where the waitresses were tending to the other customers' drink and food orders. After another emphatic shake of Big Ed's massive noggin, the girls seemed to simmer down. Ed shuffled away as fast as his big body could carry him.

"More! More! More!" The crowd chanted and stomped their feet the way they did every night when the music stopped even for a minute.

The girls settled down and, with a few ringing notes on the piano keys, Clive started up another number. Golden wiped his forehead with the already damp rag he carried in his pocket, stretched his fingers, then poured himself back into the music.

For the length of another set, he managed to forget about the diamond girl and her glittering friends. But at the end of the set, the band scattered. Clive went off to find his girl lurking at the back of the bar, watching for any other woman ready to grab her man. Winston ran to the john to sniff whatever foolishness he had up his nose. Marley, who dressed every day in suits and ties, dipped out the back alley door to grab a smoke. Golden followed.

Instead of standing outside Rosie's back door like the customers did, Golden walked a few yards away to the awning of Swiss Jewel Emporium. The Emporium had been closed nearly a month now. In this neighborhood, it was tough for a high-class place like that, specializing in expensive watches and gems, to survive. Too bad, since Golden had liked the owners, two guys from someplace in Europe. They didn't chase him off when he came in nearly every day to gawk at the cases filled with glittering rings and necklaces. Those pretty things reminded him of his mother and her love of all things shiny.

Golden settled under the Emporium's awning with his back to the rough brick wall and a cigarette in his hand. He stiffened at the sound of footsteps and only relaxed when Marley made herself comfortable just a couple of feet away. He didn't tell her to kick off. As social as she could be, Marley had her own reasons for keeping away from the crowd gathered at Rosie's back door.

Golden was fresh to the city and still trying to get the hang of this smoking thing. Damn near everybody, including Clive, who he'd known back in Opal, said that real city men smoked. Golden didn't see the sense in it, but he had to admit it gave him the excuse to step away from the crowd and sit in his own quiet for a while. He still wasn't used to the rush and noise of the city, of people everywhere and the near-constant clang and clatter of his too-close neighbors. Sometimes, it was just too much. Although he was pushed out of Opal at the threat of a noose for looking at a white girl—which was bull because he preferred his girls as black as his coffee—Golden missed home.

He still longed for those quiet Southern evenings, nights of glow bugs and cicadas and the full moon burning a clear path across a field of peach trees. Seven months and he still yearned for all those things like crazy. But he wasn't returning to Georgia. He had a plan, and it didn't include moving backward.

"I'm heading to the john." Marley tossed her cigarette butt into a nearby puddle. Just before they'd got to the club that night, the rain had come and gone in a flash and left the streets wet but the skies clear.

"All right," Golden said, rolling his still-unlit cig between two fingers. "See you inside."

After Marley took off, Golden tucked the cig into the corner of his mouth and leaned into the bumpy bricks at his back. He loosened his muscles one at a time and breathed out around the cigarette, long and deep.

These days, it seemed to take a lot of work for him to relax.

He'd only just closed his eyes when the sound of raindrops drew him back to the present and into the musty alley. He looked up. From under the protection of the awning, the rain was almost nice. If the idea of walking back to his place in the rain and mud didn't threaten to ruin his one good pair of suit pants, he'd like it more.

Still, it was hard to be mad when a piece of the South visited him in the city like this. Light raindrops falling from the sky, lit by the streetlamps, aglow and surreal.

"That's not how you smoke a cigarette, you know."

The alley wasn't dark, but it was long, just a narrow strip between the building that housed Rosie's and the Emporium on one side and a combination liquor/department store on the other.

A woman walked toward Golden. It seemed like she materialized out of the air. She wore white and floated through the sprinkles of rain with an unlit smoke of her own held between long fingers. The diamond girl.

Golden almost swallowed his cigarette. It was only when he was fumbling to keep it from going down his throat that he heard a flurry of giggling conversation near Rosie's. What the hell? Two other girls stood between him and Rosie's door. They didn't look like they belonged anywhere near an alley. They watched him and Diamond Girl.

She came closer.

"Light me up?" Diamond Girl held the cig under her chin, protecting it from the raindrops sprinkling over her hair and pretty white dress.

The chain from a watch glinted gold against the dress and disappeared into a small pocket at her waist. The sight of her away from the noise and crowd punched him in the chest.

God *damn*, she was pretty.

Fighting breathlessness, Golden fumbled in his pocket for the silver match safe he hadn't yet pulled out for himself. He lit one of the matches with a flick of his fingernail and lifted the flame to the cig already at the girl's dark red lips. She sucked on the white stem of the cig. The tip flared red. In the combined glow from the lit cigarette and the street lamps, her skin looked dangerously soft.

Damn. Just...damn.

No way a woman should be that good looking and not be in a magazine, or a museum.

A smile blossomed on her face, like she knew what he was thinking. Blowing a plume of smoke to the side, she took the glowing cig from her mouth. "That's how you smoke, baby," she said.

He took the one out of his mouth, held it between two fingers, and looked down at it like it had done him some wrong. "It's not really my thing, anyway," he said. "Cigarettes make my mouth taste like ashes."

"Like ashes?" With the burning cig in one hand, elbow bent and balanced in the palm of her other hand, she quirked her moist lips. "What about my mouth, would it taste like ashes, too?"

Shock and a sudden blast of desire shot up Golden's spine. But while his brain was wrecked at the very thought of sipping from her rosy lips, his mouth opened up to save him. "Probably, and it's not a flavor I'm fond of," he said. "No matter where it's coming from."

The quality of the woman's smile changed, becoming less flirty and more flinty, like she'd taken his rejection to taste the cigarette from her mouth personally.

"You're not from around here, are you?" Just like before, she didn't wait for his response. She raised her voice. "Sounds like you just fell off a peach truck fresh from down South."

His fingers tightened around the unlit cigarette. Did this woman just...?

A rush of heat, part humiliation but mostly anger, scorched him from head to toe. Golden knew if they'd been in the bright sun, she would have been able to see every shade of furious red rushing under his pale yellow skin.

Giggles from her friends scurried at him like small spiders.

Golden shoved the match safe in his pocket hard enough to feel a seam break. "I come from somewhere it's considered uncouth and low class to be rude." He looked down at her from his height of just over six feet and realized, even in the midst of his anger, she was only a few inches shorter than he was, the perfect height for kissing.

Snarling at himself, he tucked the limp cigarette behind his ear and stalked toward the entrance of Rosie's, ignoring the pair of brightly dressed girls who gawked at him and giggled some more.

"Did you lose your catch, Leonie?" A woman's teasing voice rolled down the alley and followed him into the dance hall. One of Diamond Girl's friends.

Golden had always been a laid-back guy and never liked it when folks flew off the handle because somebody said something they didn't like. But, damn it if he didn't understand why they got so mad. Nothing made him more ornery than somebody treating him like an idiot just because he was from down South. Especially other Negroes.

Inside Rosie's, he waded through the press of hot bodies and the smell of booze to hop back on the stage.

"What's the word with the hot piece that followed you out to the alley?" Clive closed his fancy cigarette case and put a smoke between his lips. Like most people, he smoked inside the club. He didn't need the same escape Golden did. "She looked hot for you, that's for sure."

"Nobody followed me anywhere. The girl was just getting some air with her friends."

"Didn't look like it to me."

"Seems like you better get your eyes checked then." He tried to make a joke of it with a slap to Clive's skinny shoulder.

Winston and Marley had already returned to the stage and were settling in. Marley tossed back her last swallow of liquor and slid the glass over the floor, out of everybody's way. At the front of the stage, she cleared her throat, getting ready.

"Let's make this money so I can go home with my girl," Winston said.

He wasn't the only one hoping to catch the slippery fish of success at the end of the line. Golden had his eye on bigger things, too. His dreams didn't end here in the nation's capital, where the colored help could play music all night long on stage but weren't allowed to sit at a table and enjoy the show with everyone else. Those whites-only places bothered him more than all the others. Here, Negroes like him were good enough to entertain but not human enough to deserve their own entertainment.

"Yeah," Clive said with a snicker. "And maybe Golden boy, here, can get that girl out there who's been eyeing him all night."

Golden snorted and grabbed his banjo. He played a few bars to warm up his fingers and then dove into the sweet shelter of his music. In front, the jewel girls sat at their fancy table, obviously eyeing him, but he managed to ignore them for the rest of the night.

In bed, much later that night, it was another story.

Diamond Girl found him in his dreams.

There, she was an ebony goddess with fire-red lips who hovered over him and teased him with her body. When she kissed him, she left the taste of ashes on his tongue. Golden woke up twisted in his sheets, his chest and belly heaving and damp with sweat from the lustful labor of his dreams. He burned.

His entire body was a hard and hungry ache not even the crude touch of his own hand could satisfy. A short while later, with the slick of his release drying on his hand and belly, he panted roughly at the ceiling.

If he never saw that girl again, it would be too soon.

2
———

Saturday night.

Rosie's was more packed than usual, at least as far as Golden could tell. People drank, they argued, they danced.

The night started rough. Winston and his girl got into it on the walk to the club from the two-room place they shared. The argument didn't end at Rosie's door, not by Winston's choice. His girl was loud and flashed a knife, threatening to cut off his privates. When she brought the knife with her through the doors of the bar, still threatening Winston, Big Ed brought the hammer down. He threw out the girl *and* Winston. Now they were a band member short, and on the day Clive wanted to try something new that heavily involved the trumpet, an instrument Winston played well.

"God dammit!" For once, the usually even-keeled Clive was upset. "Why doesn't that man just leave the crazies alone?"

"You know," Marley rasped in her cigarette-roughened voice, "he says the cracked ones are the best in the sheets." She'd taken Winston's usual seat behind the drums and looked real comfortable.

"His pecker isn't doing me any favors tonight," Clive muttered.

Golden couldn't resist. "Not him, either."

So they were a man short. No problem. Nothing was getting in the way of Golden making his living in this newfangled city, and, eventually, out of it.

"I can play the trumpet, you know that," he said.

"Yeah, but who's gonna pluck away on your damn banjo, a ghost?" A vein throbbed in Clive's forehead. "We need both parts."

It went without saying that Marley would pick up any slack on the drums if needed.

"Let's just work something out that won't make us sound like complete idiots. We've done better with worse." Golden nudged his friend like old times. "Come on."

Being in Washington together had been strangely hard on their friendship. They'd been better connected and better friends during the four years Golden was still in Opal and Clive was making a way for himself in the city. Between his regular gig at Rosie's and his job as a dishwasher at Joe's, Golden didn't have much of a social life, which meant he barely got the chance to see his friend. He barely got the chance to do much of anything.

Now, his friend watched him with calculating eyes.

Then Clive said, "All right. We'll put you on it and see what happens. The first number is as usual, so you stick with the banjo and what we usually do, I'll signal which one. Second number, put your banjo down and grab the horn." He handed Golden the sheet music. "Take a look."

The change was simple enough, but good. Golden and the trumpet were damn near best friends. He could play it in his sleep. When Clive invited him into the band, though, there had only been room for a banjo, another so-called country boy doing his thing. It was one of the four instruments Golden played.

"Nothing doin', my man." Golden went to get everything ready.

In the end, the show was damn good.

By the mid-evening break, Golden was sweating like a whore in church from playing the banjo and dancing in his chair. But once he got the trumpet in his hands, it was like coming home. His whole body moved with the music and he barely had to look down at the sheet music. More than once, Golden gave in to his natural inclination to improvise, and that made the rag pulse with a wild energy. Blowing hard and fast, his trumpet flirted with the beat of the African drums and Clive's bullying piano. It was damn amazing.

Rosie's thundered with applause and the stamping of feet after the last number. The band did a long encore of the last two songs, hot with the drums and the wailing sex of the trumpet, and their music opened the floodgates to writhing and jiving bodies on the dance floor. Even those regulars who didn't normally dance were shaking their black bottoms to the music. The crowd loved it so much, they barely let the band off the stage.

In the thrill of it, Golden laughed like a madman. At intermission, people plucked at their clothes and hands, begging them to get back up there and wind them up some more. They did three encores before finally shouting, "Enough!"

They put their instruments away and the crowd flooded toward the bar to take advantage of last call.

"Damn, that was good!" Golden slapped Clive hard on the back and his skinny friend almost fell over, but Golden kept him up upright with a grip on his loosened shirttails. They both laughed.

Clive knew his music, and he knew his way around business too. He was always switching things up at Rosie's. Even when something was working real good, he wasn't afraid to take a chance on something new. Which, Golden thought, was why he hadn't been too broken up when the previous banjo player got into trouble and had to skip town lickety-split ahead of the cops.

"Yeah." Clive mopped his face and returned the gesture, this time adding a quick hug. "You were magic, man. Absolute magic." It was his way of saying Golden's idea to play both instruments had been a good one.

"What am I, chopped liver?" Marley grumbled with a playful smile.

Golden laughed. "Never that." He gave her a quick hug, too. She'd played the drums liked she damn well *owned* them.

When Marley walked off to get her pay for the night, Golden jumped off the stage and left Clive excitedly eying his music notes and puffing on a cigarette. His friend was too keyed up to take a break now, even to eat. Golden wasn't hungry, but he needed out of the smoke- and perfume-filled air. He needed to breathe.

Once he was outside and leaning against the Emporium's wall, he toyed with the cigarette behind his ear but didn't put it in his mouth.

It was a dry night. The clouds that had rolled through during the day had already passed on without leaving any rain behind. Golden was grateful for that. He'd spent too much of the night before washing the mud and dirt from the bottom of his slacks just so he could hang them to dry and get ready for another night at Rosie's. The clothes smelled like smoke, but it wasn't like they weren't going right back into the stink the next night, and the one after that.

"I found you again."

That unforgettable voice brought his eyes up from their contemplation of the ground. Diamond Girl.

Tonight, her dress was yellow. It was a pale shade that made her pretty skin glow under the street lamps. Her head was bare again, black hair thick and shiny around her heart-stopping face. The dress wasn't tight, but it hugged her well enough for him to have a pretty good idea how she looked without it on. Like a sleek animal of the hunt. One of a kind.

Golden tried not to notice, but he was only a man. Cruel or not, Diamond Girl was the prettiest thing he'd ever seen, woman or jewel. The shine of her in the night was made for a man to run his hands over. He felt like Midas, but instead of gold, his lust was for diamonds.

But they were too cold for someone like him.

"I'm not exactly hard to track down," Golden said in response to her greeting. He made his voice hard, hoping she'd get to the point of why she'd followed him out here again.

A quick glance around showed only some regulars from the club, Marley chatting with a few hookers who occasionally stopped by the bar before heading off to their late night work. None of Diamond Girl's jewel-bright friends.

She had a cigarette again. Unlit and held in the same position as the night before. Déjà vu.

"Can I get a light?" she asked.

Golden fingered the silver match safe in his pocket. "I got nothing for you tonight, honey."

The smallest of frowns dropped between her elegant brows. Damn, he wished he could stop noticing how pretty she was. After that moment of almost-hurt on her face, she flicked her cigarette into the shadows. "Fine." A waste of tobacco. "That's not why I'm out here, anyway."

"Then?"

"I..." Diamond Girl bit her top lip, rolling it between sharp, white teeth.

His eyebrows shot up. Uncertainty was an interesting look on her. Unusual.

A girl like her had no reason to hesitate. From where Golden stood, she had everything she wanted in life: money, friends, privilege, and the good fortune not to be born in the South. Standing in the shadows of a failed jewelry business while roughs and whores cursed within hearing distance didn't seem like something she would do. Not unless there was a bet or the approval of her giggling friends at stake.

A sigh, and a shift of her sleek frame. "I'm sorry about last night," she finally said.

"Okay."

She frowned again and the uncertainty vanished. "Okay? That's all you're going to say?"

"Do you want a cookie?"

Her hands landed on her hips, and the look on her face became seriously pissed instead of close to sorry. He almost laughed at the quick turnaround. This wasn't a woman who apologized often, if at all. "Why are you making it hard for me to say I'm sorry?"

"Because your sorry is as fake as Rosie's hair." He jerked his head toward the dance hall and the owner's famous waist-length locks.

Silence between them cracked as loud as a gunshot. While they'd talked, she wandered closer. The glow of her skin, the fit of her dress, the rose of her mouth blossoming in the lush midnight garden of her face mesmerized him.

God damn if her hoity-toity ways weren't turning him into some sort of lust-drunk poet. Golden had to shake himself to get loose from her spell.

She was just another bored rich girl trying to toy with him for a night's fun. He needed her to be gone, and he needed to get back into the club. He pushed off the wall and tucked away his cigarette.

"What do I have to do to convince you I'm sorry?" A familiar note of seduction crept into her voice, and she moved closer to him. Did she really want a man trophy so badly?

Too busy nursing his mother through her final days, Golden may not have made time with as many women as Clive, but it was obvious as hell what she was on about.

Diamond Girl snaked even closer to him, lashes falling low over melting brown eyes, pink tongue flicking once over her ruby lips. Her perfume elevated the alley to a garden of temptation. Every other scent was gone except for whatever was on her skin, in her hair. All the other sounds disappeared. The voices down the way, the whine of the industrial fan at Rosie's that barely moved around the otherwise stale air. It was just him and Diamond Girl and the lust he felt rising in his spine, settling low in his belly.

But she didn't want him. It was all an act. A play for the entertainment of her friends.

Golden sighed. Suddenly, he was just tired. "You don't have to do that."

"Do what?" The words whispered across her lips like a filthy promise. Another lie.

His fingers jerked and crushed the cigarette in his pocket. "See you around." Golden turned his back and walked away from her. Again. He strolled into Rosie's feeling dirty. Even worse than the night before, when Diamond Girl had dismissed him. He'd never met anyone like her, never mind anyone with her distracting beauty. Why did she keep coming close to him? Her cold and heat scalded him and left him wound up tight. Frustrated.

But something about tonight's encounter left him feeling almost sad for her. His anger was there, all right, simmering beneath the surface of his lust.

What was missing in Diamond Girl's life that made her follow him around like this? He was nothing but a country bumpkin still rolling from the fall off a peach truck, he imagined she would say. She obviously needed something. Whatever it was, she needed to get it from someplace else and leave him the hell alone.

Alone. Damn.

Since leaving Opal, wasn't he always alone?

In Washington, he had only one real friend. Clive. But no one really close to him. Definitely no one who cared enough to pull a knife on him, like Winston's psycho girl. At least when she wasn't trying to kill him, Winston and her were lovey-dovey to the point of being downright sickening. Kissing and fetching drinks for each other, neatening each other's clothes and being generally sweet. Golden had left whatever he ever had of that behind in Georgia.

Diamond Girl and her antics only made him realize even more how much he didn't have.

Golden growled through his sadness and continued toward the stage. He was halfway there when Marley gestured to Clive, then pointed at Golden. Clive jumped off the stage and headed his way.

"Hey, man. I've been looking for you!" Clive's brief grip on his arm snagged his attention.

"What are you talking about? I was in the same place I am every night."

"Yeah, yeah." He raised his voice even more above the noise. "A guy's here. He really likes your music and wants to talk to you."

Clive was acting strange, even for him. Golden hesitated. "About what?"

"You'll see. Come on." Clive guided him through the crowd and into one of the small back rooms that served as offices at Rosie's.

"Found him," Clive said.

In the office, a guy sat on top of the single desk smoking a thin cigar. The chair in front of the desk was empty, but Rosie took up the entire faded couch, decorated in red and white roses, smoking a cigar of her own. The hair she'd bought and paid for lay braided over her shoulder like a sleeping snake. She toyed with it and sucked on her cigar while she talked with the stranger. Their conversation cut off when Clive and Golden walked into the room.

"Nice job," the guy said. He was dark as night, the lit end of the cigar glowing around his face, making his deep-set eyes squint against the smoke. He jumped off the desk. "I'm Nelson Biggers. Good to finally meet you, Golden Boy!" He stuck out his hand to shake.

"It's Golden," Golden said, firmly taking the offered hand. He may be pretty and light-skinned, but he was nobody's *boy*. Not even to another Negro. "Golden Worth."

Nelson grinned. "All right, *Golden*." He placed particular emphasis on the name as the corners of his eyes crinkled with some private amusement. "Just to let you know, though, your mama didn't do you any favors naming a yellow-eyed, yellow boy like you after something that's bought and sold."

Golden didn't bother giving him the usual line about gold being valued for itself alone. It was a greedy man, and a white man at that, who put a price on gold, lusted after it, and made it the root of the destruction of entire civilizations.

"What can I do for you, Nelson?" Since the man hadn't used Golden's last name, he returned the favor.

"It's more of what I can do for you, Golden. I heard you play out there. Fantastic!" He waved his lit cigarette around like a baton. "I work with some guys in Europe—France, in particular, Marseilles. They'd especially just love to have a guy like you in their band. I've been over here looking, and you're the first guy I've seen who's really worth something." The corners of his eyes crinkled again in amusement just as Clive shifted at Golden's side, obviously irritated by the comment.

"Don't lay it on so thick," Clive said to Nelson. "Get to the point. We gotta start the next set in two shakes."

From the couch, Rosie nodded and blew a set of smoke rings in the air. "Yeah, get to it."

"I already got to my point. Your boy—Golden—is a damn master. You say he plays four instruments, not just the two I saw today? Come on!" He turned to Golden. "You should think about coming to France and playing with the band in Marseilles. I'll pay your fare there, of course, and you can see what it's all about. It's a different deal from over here."

A wild hope began to pound in Golden's chest. "Different how?"

Nelson nodded toward Clive. "I heard things here don't sit so well with you. That Negroes aren't allowed to play music in certain places that pay real good. And the places you can play, you can't go into and have a drink or check out the dames on your day off. Clive was telling me that sticks in your craw real good."

"But isn't that everyone?" Golden said. "Clive cares about it, too." But he knew Clive had a girl in the city, a whole life he didn't want to give up.

"Yeah, but he wants to work the system here, maybe change it, maybe push things to the limits of what these people allow. You, though..." And he looked like he really did know what Golden wanted.

Golden had struggled like hell in Georgia, first with his father running off and leaving his mother still mourning the last of five still-born babies. Then his mother falling ill, then him taking care of her from the first fainting spell to the lowering her coffin into the grave. The whole time, he'd also struggled against a system of racism and injustice that threatened to leave him hanging from one of the magnolia trees in the town he used to love.

Goddamn, he was tired of struggling. He wanted some peace. He wanted to be his own man, on his own terms.

Rosie tipped her head up at him through the smoke from her cigar. From her presence, he knew she wouldn't make trouble for him if he decided to leave.

Golden crossed his arms over his chest and tried to be cool, even though his heart pounded hard enough to burst through his clothes. "All right," he said. "I'm listening."

3

A fter his meeting with Nelson Biggers, the rest of Golden's night went by in a fog.

What the man offered was out of this world—*if* he and the offer were for real. Golden had dealt with enough con men to be suspicious of someone offering up something that seemed too good to be true:

Leave this place of limited opportunities. Play his music in any club he wanted. Make more money. Stretch beyond the square-box life *this* country had put him in.

It sounded damn good. But was it *too* good?

He jingled the loose change in his pocket and stepped out into the darkness of Washington, D.C. sometime after four in the morning. Although he was normally a careful guy, he hardly paid attention to his surroundings on his short walk to the little one-room set-up above Joe's restaurant. Home. Nelson's offer bopped back and forth in his brain.

The night was cool for summer, meaning it wasn't threatening to melt his skin from his bones. He took a shortcut through an alley behind the shop and stopped under a streetlight to fish his keys out of his pocket and breathe deep and easy before walking into his place. If he kept up these frantic what-if's, he wouldn't be able to sleep through the night.

A slight movement behind him in the otherwise dark street yanked him around. But he didn't see anyone. After a brief hesitation, he kept going to his place. He kept his hands loose at his sides and his steps unhurried.

At the heavy door two steps up from the pavement, he undid the lock and shoved the door open, keeping the keys in his hand. He went up the first step and then the second, keeping the door slightly open, the steep stairs leading up to his rooms at his back. When a slim shadow unwound from the street lamp, he was ready for it. What he wasn't ready for was the *source* of the shadow.

"Funny seeing you here," Diamond Girl said. She looked completely comfortable standing on a mostly dark street with a strange man.

Was she out of her mind? Golden's mouth tightened with irritation. "Quit playing around and following me. This is getting crazy."

"I want to talk to you," she said, shimmering on the dark and deserted street.

Her pretty yellow dress alone looked like it was worth at least a hundred dollars. The lace along the high collar was fine and delicate, and he would bet his night's pay that the buttons fastening the cloth down her slim throat and between her breasts were real pearls. Golden jerked his gaze back up to her face.

"You seem to want a lot of things," he said, then realized he could've been talking about himself.

"You never accepted my apology." She slid closer and her hand braced the door open, one elegantly booted foot perching on the second step. "But I suppose I really didn't give you one." Despite her nearly aggressive move into his personal space, her gestures were delicate, nothing like the girls he was used to at home. Those girls' bodies, mostly hardened by life and circumstances, were feline and graceful. Predatory in a way meant to lure, then tear apart.

Darkness softened the unreal beauty of Diamond Girl's face. Her perfume was potent, even under the layers of smoke and the evening's sweat. The desire to sweep his tongue over her warm skin and taste her salty sweat and bitter perfume nearly overcame him. Golden licked his lips.

"I really am sorry," she said.

He clenched his teeth. What game was she playing? "Fine, I'll accept your apology," he said. "But, damn, you're spoiled."

"Why, because I can't get your pretty eyes out of my mind?"

Golden rolled the eyes she mentioned. He'd heard similar compliments plenty of times. In Opal, the old white slave masters and landowners had had their way with so many of the girls back in the day that most people in the town were probably related. Pale brown eyes like his were like sand on the beach.

"No," he finally said to the girl. "Because you don't take my 'no' for an answer."

"I just don't want you to think badly of me."

"Too late for that."

She flinched and actually looked hurt. But it didn't last long. "Okay, fine. So I tried."

"Yeah, you did."

Her pretty mouth pinched at the corners and she backed away down the steps. "It isn't just about your eyes, you know. You play music really well. I forgot to tell you, with all the—" She made a motion with a slender hand, then fingered the chain of her pocket watch. "Anyway, have a pleasant evening, and maybe I'll see you again at the club sometime."

Then she turned away and slipped back into the shadows.

Good riddance.

Golden continued on up to his apartment. He locked the door behind him, then left his hat on the rack by the door with his jacket. He emptied the change from his pants pockets, dropped his night's pay and tips into the coffee can he kept on his bookshelf next to the photograph of his mother.

Diamond Girl fluttered in his mind like a troublesome blue jay caught on a string.

Shit.

Cursing some more, he grabbed his keys, locked the door behind him, and jogged back down the stairs. A woman like that had no business wandering around by herself this time of night. She was spoiled and just plain trouble, but he was also too much of a Southern gentleman to allow her to make her way home alone.

Just watch and see. You'll feel real stupid when you go out there and see her ride off in a private car with her friends.

But that thought didn't stop him from rushing into the street to find her.

The night felt darker than when he'd first gone to his room, menacing in a way he hadn't felt before. But he didn't feel the worry for himself. Alarm nagged at him with each street he turned and didn't see a sign of Diamond Girl's pale dress, no hint of that dark cloud of hair or her swaying walk.

He took the way he knew most people went between his street and Rosie's. Then he remembered…. Shit, of course. She'd followed him. And he'd rambled through an alley he didn't normally go down because of the toughs who tended to hang out there and smoke.

He wasn't afraid of them, but one against three or four weren't great odds, especially when he didn't want to get his work clothes dirty. Earlier, he'd walked through the alley with his mind someplace else, which was stupid. Those guys were bad enough in the light of day, but even worse after dark. The night gave even the most cowardly bastard the courage to do what he didn't feel quite up to during the day.

Golden doubled back to the alley, hoping the girl had more sense than to walk through it.

"Try it and I'll slash your face!"

The gasped words, bravely tinged with a hint of fear, hurried him into the alley. What he saw there made the blood freeze in his veins. Diamond Girl was backing slowly away from three toughs, her figure a rigid line, her chin lifted in a challenge. She slashed a knife—a goddamn knife—in the air in front of her, weaving it toward the three guys, all younger than her but fierce like jackals.

This part of town was a mix of everybody, and this gang of toughs showed that. A tow-headed idiot with pale eyes and a gap-toothed grimace elbowed the guy next to him, a high yellow fella with thick curls down his back like a woman. They both signaled their friend, Italian-looking with muscles all over the place, to get closer to the girl.

They came at her in a circle, the Italian grinning with all his teeth, the other two slow, like they had all the time in the world. They backed her into a filthy wall smelling of piss and other things Golden didn't want to put names to. Fear for her lurched in his stomach.

"Oh, honey, you must really like us. This foreplay is real nice." The grinning one laughed now. "But you want to see mine?" He flicked out a switchblade.

Golden took it all in within seconds. The boys barely looked up at him, keeping their gazes focused on Diamond Girl. Good.

"You don't want any of this, friend." A boy Golden didn't notice before spoke from a darkened corner.

Dammit.

Diamond Girl flicked a panicked glance Golden's way, the first hint of her worry. That was when the grinning one lunged toward her. Then he howled in pain and jerked back, his knife clattering to the ground as dark blood gushed from his wrist.

"You bitch!"

With a growl, Golden threw himself into the fight. His guilt made him fiercer, anger at himself lending more power and strength to his fists as he battered down every last one of the stupid boys who dared to touch what had been offered to him.

Like most of the guys he grew up with, Golden fought dirty. But he also fought fast. No point drawing out a fight with fists when a quick kick to the nuts would bring things to a swift close. He cut through the guys like new grass, pummeling them down one by one until all he had left was the Italian who danced around him like he was some kind of boxer, deftly keeping out of range of Golden's fists and feet, his teeth glinting in the dark. This bastard better—

A feminine shriek of pain spiked anger and worry through him, and he spared a precious second to look the girl's way. Blood dripped from the arm she held tight against her body. She'd lost her hat in the fight, probably her knife, too. But the guy who cut her was on the ground and curled into himself, desperately trying to avoid the deadly aim of her booted feet. She kicked him again and again, grunting and cursing.

A fist slammed into Golden's jaw, drawing his attention back to where it needed it to be.

Time to end this.

He jumped back, out of range of the guy's fists, then dipped low and darted in, slamming his fist into the guy's crotch. With a high squeal, his attacker dropped like a tree, his eyes round with shock and pain. He curled up like a roly-poly on the dirty ground, but that was all Golden stayed around to see. He grabbed Diamond Girl's uninjured arm.

"Come on!"

She spun on him, her other arm raised, eyes fierce enough to cut. "Let—!" But when she saw it was him, she sagged in relief and cradled her arm against her stomach once again.

"No time for that, let's go." They could rest when they weren't anywhere near these guys. They were down for now, but they weren't guaranteed to stay that way.

Her eyes narrowed. "Not without my knife!"

Golden scooped the fancy-looking piece from the ground and gave it back to her. Quickly, she slid the knife into the little cloth purse dangling from her wrist.

"Let's go!" he said again.

He hustled her through the alley, to his front door, and up the narrow stairs to his room. He gave her a gentle shove toward the bed and locked the door behind them.

The sound of their heavy breathing huffed in the room.

Goddamn....

While he caught his breath, Diamond Girl dropped down onto his bed. She held her hand still against her stomach, and in the light from the lantern he'd stupidly forgot to dampen on his way out, her skin looked nearly gray. Blood from her slashed arm leaked out sluggishly.

He swallowed one last hurried breath and licked his dry lips. "Let me clean that for you."

"It's fine," she said, although her eyes flared with more than a hint of worry. "I'll just wait until I get home to have my—someone look at it."

Was she about to say her nanny or butler?

"There's no point being proud just so an infection can take your whole hand off."

He dragged out an old-fashioned leather bag one of his friends had found and gifted to him as a joke, saying Golden needed to learn how to doctor himself since he got into so many fights.

He put the bag on the bed next to her, then left with a metal bowl to fetch some clean water from the shared bathroom down the hall.

When he came back, the girl was ripping the pale yellow cloth of her dress away from her bleeding cut while her teeth bit into her lower lip. A frown of concentration settled between her brows.

She looked up. "I thought it would hurt much worse being cut up in a knife fight."

He gestured to her little scratch. "If you think this is being cut up, you have a lot to learn about knife fights." Although he'd rather her not learn anything more. At least, not while he was nearby. With the bowl of water safely on the floor, he grabbed a stool and sat it down close to the bed.

"Give me your arm."

She flicked a look at him, a hint of nervousness, before putting her arm across his palm.

He couldn't help but notice how delicate and slender her arm was in his broad hand, but the fine tremor in it quickly reminded him of why he was touching her in the first place.

With efficient movements he'd learned from his mother, he cleaned the shallow two-inch cut and washed it out with some whiskey. He expected her to cry out when the alcohol splashed in the wound, but a muscle clenched in her jaw, a hiss of breath left her parted lips. That was it.

If it had been him, he'd have been bawling like a goddamn baby. Golden looked up at her with admiration, but her gaze was trained on what his hands were doing, lashes low over her eyes.

He wrapped her arm with gauze and a bandage, fitting it all tightly so it wouldn't bleed through the dress.

He rested her arm on a clean piece of cloth he draped over his thigh. He heard the thick sound of her swallowing and smelled the richness of her perfume, seasoned by the day's sweat. His heart was wild in his chest, beating faster than Winston's drums.

He forced his hands steady. Although he was tempted, he didn't do anything more than tend to the wound marring the smoothness of her arm. He did forgive himself, though, for his lingering touch on her dress that, for all its glitter, was surprisingly soft. He felt every exhale of her breath as she leaned close, every inhale of his own. They were both breathing hard by the time he was done.

"That's really good," she said, looking down at the bandage and not at him. "How did you learn to do that?"

"We country boys are good for more than a roll in the hay," he said, washing his hands in the bowl of water and drying off with a towel.

She grabbed his arm. "I'm sorry," she said. "Seems like I'm always saying the wrong thing to you."

"It's not like we're going to be friends or anything. Don't worry about it."

What they should both worry about, though, was the way she looked up at him from his bed, her eyes long-lashed and soft. This was an even more appealing picture than she'd made at the club the first time he saw her surrounded by her friends. More appealing, and more dangerous. Everything about her look invited him to kiss her.

And because she was there in the very same room, in the very same *bed* where he'd dreamt of her, and because she was leaning close with her sweet salt scent, and because he was just plain weak,

Golden kissed her. She slipped a hand up his chest and kissed him right back.

Damn. Her lips were as luscious as he'd imagined. They parted for him just like in his dreams, cool and soft. She sighed and pressed into him and, just like that, he was lost.

It would have been different if she'd pushed him, tried to move him around like she'd done those boys in the alley, like she'd tried to do to him at Rosie's. But she yielded her soft body to him in a way that sparked him like gasoline. Her fingers pressed into the back of his neck, and he groaned like a man felled from the height of the tallest pecan tree.

Not a good idea. Not a good idea at all.

But those thoughts didn't stop him from slicking her mouth with his tongue, licking past the plump temptation of her slightly parted lips to get at the taste he knew lay just inside. Wet. And sweet. It didn't seem fair when she moaned again and slid even closer.

Golden pushed to his feet, vaguely aware of the bowl of water on the floor and the now damp rag falling from his thigh. None of those things mattered. Just her warmth and the hot huff of surprise from her lips when he stood, looping an arm around her waist, bringing her up with him.

Lips to lips, belly to belly. The soft temptation of her scent all around him.

Yes, there was the copper smell of blood. But it grounded him in a moment that was real, that he had never thought to associate with someone like her, with her shiny dresses and expensive perfume.

He wanted her. The wet heat of her mouth and the sweet way she kissed him back, meeting him hunger for hunger, harsh breath for harsh breath. These things told him she wanted him, too. It wasn't to impress her friends. Well, maybe it *was* to prove to herself she could get a fresh-off-the-peach-truck country hick to fall into her lap. But, damn, it didn't even matter.

She was a woman, soft against him, and he was a man, hard against her. If this was what she'd wanted the moment she sought him out in the alley, then goddamn, all she'd had to do was say so in the first place.

His blood beat hot and fast enough in his veins to scorch him from head to toe. Groaning low and deep, he dug his hands into her waist. Caught up in his lust, Golden pushed her back into the bed. She went willingly, knees bending, sighs seductive and soft. He fumbled for the fastening at the back of her dress.

She winced, and he felt the motion through their connection. He pulled back and their lips released with a filthy, wet sound.

"Are you all right?" He gasped the question, so worked up he was this close to making a mess in his pants.

"Yes...yes." Her hands slid over his chest, pushing under his shirt. "Just kiss me."

But with that small bit of space between them, Golden could see she was hurting. The pain from her little knife fight was catching up with her. He pulled all the way back.

"No," he said. "You're hurt. I was stupid for trying to force myself on you."

"You didn't force anything." She sat up until they were practically chest to chest, her soft breasts pillowed against him, her breath huffing against his chin. "You didn't hear me screaming, did you?"

With her melting eyes on his, she raked her fingernails over his chest. He shivered and his cock pulsed. If she looked down, she wouldn't have been able to miss the pike in his trousers. But she kept her eyes on his face, seducing him with the pure sex in her eyes and the even strokes of her nails on his skin.

Christ....

He swallowed and forced the words past his throat. "Maybe you weren't screaming, but you're still hurt."

She looked at him with her dark, swirling eyes and a faint line pressed between her brows. Her fingers, as light as butterfly wings, fluttered up and down his chest and belly. "You're serious, aren't you?"

"Why wouldn't I be?" Although if she kept on touching him, he'd forget all about her pain, and make her forget about it, too, with a deep application of a time-honored cure.

She leaned up to kiss him again, but he stopped her with a grip on her arms.

"Why do you have to be the most honorable man in all of Washington?" She groaned. But there was a tease, too, a smile, and she didn't protest again when he sat back on his heels.

"Let me get you some medicine for the pain."

She looked at him with that same smile, a little puzzled and a lot intrigued. "Okay." She moved to sit back in the bed and winced again, looked down at her arm as if she'd forgotten the reason she was there in his bed in the first place. She cradled her bandaged arm against the other and wriggled until she sat at the edge of the bed. "It's starting to hurt a little more than before."

Very carefully, Golden took himself all the way off the bed and left for the bathroom with the bowl of water, now pink with her blood.

When he got back, she was right where he left her, sitting at the edge of his bed with the sleeve of her fancy dress torn away, cradling her arm. He gave her some pain powder dissolved in a glass of water. After a quick, suspicious glance into the glass of milky liquid, she put it to her lips and drank until it was all gone. She made a face and set the empty glass on the small table near the bed.

"That was vile," she said, making a gagging noise.

"But your pain should be gone soon enough."

The doctors had given that medicine to his mother for the pain toward the end. After, he just kept what was left over.

She rolled her eyes and stood, keeping her bandaged hand close to her stomach. "I know how aspirin works, country boy."

"So do I, city girl," he said and got out of her way, more than ever aware of the small size of his one-room place. His body, still stupidly aroused, tracked every move she made. He needed to get her out before they ended up back in bed again. If for no other reason than the lack of floor space. "Are you ready to go?"

She stopped just in front of his bed. "What's your name, anyway?

I can't keep calling you 'Country Boy' in my head. Especially since you just had your tongue down my throat." Her grin was a mischievous tease.

He felt himself pause, knew that when he did it, she would notice it and comment. "Golden," he said.

"Like your eyes."

He paused again, caught by surprise at her reaction. Most folks he'd met in Washington just told him how countrified his name sounded, and the ones at the club advised him to change it to Tom or Buster or something else so he could blend in. But he knew if it wasn't his name it would be something else they didn't like, so he figured he might as well keep the whole thing and let somebody else worry about fitting in.

"If you say so," Golden said at last. He just thought of them as light brown. Fancy women had fancy ways, he supposed. Including fanciful words to describe something that was just brown.

"I do say so." She grinned at him, and her own eyes sparkled. A dimple appeared in one cheek, unexpected and brief. "Mine is Leonie." She stuck out her hand. "Pleased to meet you."

He looked at her hand for a moment, the slenderness of it, and remembered her daring and cheerfulness after what happened to her out in the alley. Slowly, he took her hand and squeezed it. "Charmed."

She winked at him. "I can tell you're not, not yet. But you will be."

4
___

If nothing else, this Leonie was bold.

She grinned and stepped back. "I'm leaving now," she said. "I've taken up enough of your time tonight. I'm guessing you have to be at work tomorrow, at the club."

It was probably around five in the morning by now. Golden wished that was all he had to do later on. At this rate, he wasn't going to get any sleep before his shift started at Joe's. The breakfast crowd came early, and before he got started on the customers' dishes he had to deal with the pots. But he hadn't gotten Leonie away from those guys in the alley just so she could stumble back into the night and get hemmed up by somebody else.

"I do have work," he said. "You're right about that." He didn't correct her assumption that his only job was at Rosie's. "Let me at least walk you home."

"It's okay. I'm not close." She picked up her little bag, fooling with it like she was uncomfortable about something. It couldn't be about where she lived, though, because Golden had already assumed her place was some sort of mansion. Hell, even a castle. Looking at her, it was hard to believe they even existed in the same world, much less the same city. Of course, she lived a million miles away from his little fire trap.

"Yeah. Come on." He grabbed his keys. "You don't know who else is waiting for you out there right now."

"I was being stupid earlier. I should've just called for a taxi, or something. I wasn't thinking about the time."

"Or the place?" He gave her a look and could've sworn she blushed.

But she only nodded. "Or the place."

"Don't worry about it now. Unless you have some magical machine to call and arrange for a car to come and get you right outside my door, we need to take the streetcar." He mentally calculated how much money it would take to get them both to her undoubtedly ritzy address. He had enough.

"You really don't have to do this," she said.

"I don't have to do anything but play music and die. This I'm gonna do because it's the right thing." And he wasn't ready to let her out of his sight quite yet.

Her beautiful face, even her aristocratic voice and the big words she used, were growing on him. In only a few hours, he was intimately familiar with so much of her and, idiot that he was, he only wanted the intimacy to grow.

"All right, Golden." She said his name with an indulgent smile, a smile he found he didn't mind so much.

Golden silently snorted. Yeah, like he was a puppy she'd found wandering across her path and wasn't ready to let go of quite yet. In a way, it seemed they saw each other the same way. Unless he was just making this situation up to suit what he wanted. It wouldn't have been the first time.

He locked the door. Taking her arm, he guided her into the street to find the trolley heading toward her address. No, it wasn't close at all. But there was no way he would let her hop on the streetcar alone to ride so far out into the city in the threat of darkness.

They got on the back of the nearly empty car together. Golden settled next to her on the bench seat, legs spread wide, but still careful not to touch her. It was late enough that only a few people were on the trolley, most with their chins tucked against their chests as they caught a few winks before they got to where they were going.

Golden had never been that careless. The idea of falling asleep on a trolley, or anywhere in public, was about as foreign to him as Germany or France. Being alert was his default, no matter how tired he was.

The trolley rattled along the streets, past the shuttered gambling dens and dancehalls, the corner stores and the barbershops. The street lamps glowed like rows of sentinels, watching silently as they made their way through the city.

He focused on the window glass and realized Leonie was watching him. He turned toward her and she continued looking back at him, completely unashamed and unselfconscious about being caught staring.

"How long have you been in Washington?" she asked.

"A few months." He shrugged. Seven months, three weeks, and ten hours. He hadn't yet gotten what he wanted from the city, but he'd never intended for it to be his last stop, either.

"You don't like it," she said. It wasn't a question.

"It's all right enough. People treat each other like garbage here. It's not what I'm used to." Then he had to laugh, rueful and embarrassed, remembering the reason he was here in the first place. Maybe it wasn't such a bad thing that people in Washington didn't treat him like they had back home. If that were the case, he'd be six months or more in the grave by now. "Still, city folks have an interesting way about them."

"Really? How?" She sat sideways on the bench, watching him with an almost childlike interest, focusing on him completely. Did she expect him to tell her how interesting she was? If so, she was going to be waiting a long time. Still, there was no use keeping his truth from her.

"Like you," he said, and she perked up a little.

"Me?"

"Yeah. You come up to me, a stranger, a strange *man*, wanting

God-knows-what from me. Wanting it so bad, you come to my house to get it. Another man, a worse one, might take that to mean something else altogether."

Her lashes fell low over her dark eyes and she tilted her head to look up at him. "What if I wanted you to take it that way?" The flash of white teeth between her parted and slightly pink lips tightened his stomach.

"But why? You don't even know me. I could hurt you."

"Sometimes people who know you are the ones who hurt you the most," she said, then did the thing with her lashes again. "You have kind eyes, and it's not just the gold in them."

Cradling her injured arm close to her stomach, she leaned closer as she spoke. Being with her in that moment was so much like falling. Leonie talked about his eyes, but hers were like the night sky, swirling with stars and an intriguing darkness he'd never seen before. In anyone.

"Careful you're not just seeing what you want to see," he said. "Not every pair of different-colored eyes has good things hidden in them." He'd seen plenty of folks get taken in by the light brown eyes in Opal. Captured and duped and discarded, lured in by the hypnotizing remnants of the white man who had raped the first slave way back in his line.

"I'm not looking at just any man," Leonie said with her confident, unbreakable stare. "I'm looking at you." And she was looking her fill, up close and personal, inviting what his mama called private sin.

Leonie was temptation in the flesh. Nothing he'd ever thought he'd run into in this city. He didn't know quite what to do about her, but his body knew what it wanted, tightening, hardening, getting ready for her. He deliberately didn't adjust his sprawl in the seat, allowed the rise of interest at the front of his pants to show, almost disappointed when she didn't look down. Instead, she continued to stare at his face, her tongue darting out to dance across her bottom lip. When she wet it, the motion gave him ideas that only made the problem in his lap more obvious.

"I see you're looking at me, too, Golden," she said at last.

Christ, he wanted to do more than look. But he shook himself and cleared his throat. "Is this your stop?" It was the last one, and the conductor was up front and turned around in his seat, just watching them.

"Oh!" Her eyes dipped down and she grabbed the purse already dangling from her slender wrist. "Yes, this is us." Blushing, she pulled the hem of her dress close and scrambled toward the trolley's open door.

Golden followed, but only as fast as the stiffness in his pants would let him.

They were in a neighborhood he would've never ended up in on his own in a million years. Big two- and three-level houses, tall porch columns, lawns wide enough to fit the house he'd left behind in Opal three times over. The grass in every front yard was cut low, background for fancy shrubbery, while the wide bars of high fences allowed anybody passing by a good, long look at what they didn't have.

"You were born up here?" he asked. Although he'd already known she didn't live anyplace like he did, the reality of the big houses and wide lawns, the roads that looked clean enough to eat off of and come back for seconds, was even more jarring than expected.

As they walked the long and winding street, her movements grew more and more stiff. She adjusted the torn sleeve of her dress to hide the bandage and did her best to button it closed.

Would her family worry about her being out late?

From what Leonie said earlier, she didn't live alone. She hadn't said anything about having a man; someone as bright and shiny as her seemed destined for other things, things other than a man and children. College, maybe. Working in a law office, even. He imagined her at a desk, first behind it, then leaning back on top of it, wearing her inviting smile. Golden's imagination caught on the curve of her lips giving way to her determined chin, her elegant throat, then the pretty slope of her breasts under expensive fabric. Draped over a desk, trembling for his touch.

He cleared his throat and subtly adjusted himself in his pants.

"Yes, I've lived here all my life." She walked sedately at his side, the stride of her long legs—he imagined they were long and slender and would wrap like a dream around his hips—kicking at the fabric of the dress. Her shoes clicked delicately against the sidewalk. "I expect I'll spend my last days in a house just like this one."

Golden nodded.

Years before, he would've said the same thing about the house he'd shared with his mother. It was all he'd known, and he never expected to have anything else despite wanting to do more with his music. He loved Opal and all the small things about the town that made it home. But life had changed in the blink of an eye—his mother's death, the sudden loom of the hangman's noose.

And now, here he was. Walking next to a Negro princess and fantasizing about screwing her until he knocked loose the cool and provocative mask she'd worn since the night they met. He swallowed and looked away from the sensual stride of legs under the dress.

"I'm just up there." She inclined her chin toward a house similar to all the others they passed. Tall, with a pale façade and Greek columns like soldiers guarding the red front door.

She walked even more uncomfortably now, although she was obviously trying to hide it. Her nervousness brought out the protector in him. She made him want to shield her from whatever consequences came from her following him into the dark heart of his seedy neighborhood

"Let me walk you to your door," he offered as they approached the gate.

He thought she might refuse him, but she waited while he reached past her and unlatched the tall gate. It swung open without a single squeak, well-oiled and cool under his hand, slightly damp from the early morning dew. No gate would dare do anything as common as squeak in a neighborhood like this.

Jesus. What was he doing here?

With the gate closed behind them, they headed toward the front door, the entrance glowing with light. A shape moved behind one of the windows and, moments later, the front door clicked open.

The man who stepped out onto the well-lit porch was obviously her father. Older, with thick sideburns, Leonie's dark skin, and suspiciously narrowed eyes. Although it was nearly the sunrise of a new day, he was still dressed in a full and proper suit, spit-shined shoes included. This was old money.

"Leonie Harper! Get in here."

Golden almost smiled. Even Negro princesses had to answer to someone else. Beside him, Leonie stiffened even more, but she never once stopped her forward progress toward the door. A pained smile lifted the corners of her mouth. Her arm must have been hurting.

"Papa. What are you doing up at this hour?"

"Me?" The man sputtered. Golden had to admire Leonie's boldness. "You, my daughter, are the one traipsing around Washington at all hours of the night."

It was obvious, from the way he greeted her when she rushed toward him and into his arms, that she was his favorite, maybe only, child. Or maybe he was just a man who loved his daughters enough to let them wrap him all the way around their little fingers. With Leonie in his arms, he looked over her shoulder at Golden. His eyes were cautiously hostile.

"Who is this?" he demanded. "What are you doing with him at this hour?"

Leonie pulled back from her father with a light laugh, carefully keeping her injured arm by her side and lost in the folds of her dress. "I went for a drive with the girls and they got too tired, so I ended up in town alone and this nice gentleman offered to walk me home."

There were so many holes in that lie, it was a wonder the man didn't confront Leonie on it right away. He only huffed some more and rested a hand on his daughter's shoulder. "Very well. Go on inside, then. You've had a long day and you know we have church tomorrow." He narrowed suspicious eyes at Golden.

"Yes, Papa." Leonie looked more relaxed now. Maybe she'd been worried about her father's reaction. Her lashes dropped low over her sparkling eyes and she smiled at Golden. With a quick and graceful movement, she darted from her father's side to Golden's, just close enough to touch. She offered him a hand. Not the one with the bandaged cut.

"Thank you very much, kind sir, for your escort."

Golden grunted. It was obvious she was laughing, both at him and at her father, a spoiled child who always got her way.

"You're welcome," he said, playing along. "It was good to meet you, miss. Sleep easy tonight." Golden lightly squeezed her hand, then stroked two fingers down the center of her palm, a touch he couldn't resist. Even with that limited contact, he felt her shiver.

"It was fun seeing you tonight," she said softly. "I enjoyed... everything." She cleared her throat then whirled around, quickly slipping past her father to disappear through the gleaming red doors

Golden breathed through the warmth in his chest—and his pants—that she left him with.

It was already late as hell, and if he hoped to get even an hour's sleep, he needed to get on the road. He nodded at Leonie's father, preparing to make his quick way back down the drive and disappear from their lives forever.

"Young man." Her father stepped closer with a hand extended. "Thank you for walking my daughter home. I know she's not always the easiest woman to wrangle." The old man clasped Golden's hand and Golden allowed it, but when he drew his hand back, a folded dollar bill rested in the cup of his palm.

What the hell?

"I imagine it's obvious to you what type of woman you found when you bumped into Leonie. Don't come back here and try to get anything more out of her. She doesn't have the money in this family, I do."

Humiliation crawled up Golden's cheeks in a hot, red wave. The mouth that had always gotten him in trouble at home opened up wide. At first, nothing came out, then he got it together.

"Keep your stinking money," he growled. "If I wanted something from your daughter, or even this house, I would already have it." With a sneer he felt all the way through to the soles of his feet, he dropped the money on the ground and made sure to step on it as he walked away.

"Fuckin' prick," Golden muttered.

So far, the rich Negroes had treated him just as badly as white folks down South. The way they had of looking down their noses at people who didn't have as much as they did stuck in his craw. Maybe that was how it was everywhere, but he was tired of it. And he was damn tired of Washington, too.

5

As badly as Leonie's father treated him, he couldn't get the girl out of his mind.

He didn't realize he was waiting for her to show up at Rosie's again until the disappointment settled hard in his stomach on Friday, then on Saturday night when he didn't see her face.

Golden played, he flirted, he talked with Nelson Biggers about Europe, but part of him stayed focused on the door, waiting for her familiar face. But she never came.

On Sunday, a week after he dropped her off at her doorstep, he got an unexpected day off from Joe. And, like a chump, he took the streetcar back to her neighborhood, the part of town that made the back of his neck itch.

Her place was just like he remembered. Big and rich.

The sun was fresh up in the sky and just beginning to warm the day and his skin through his good suit. He slung the jacket over his arm because, as much as he wanted to fit into the neighborhood where he planned to lurk, he didn't want to roast. It was early enough that he'd had to leave his bed at sunrise to make it here before the residents started stirring.

He didn't know why the hell he was coming to find her, but that didn't make him turn around. Smoking a cigarette, but careful to avoid inhaling the disgusting gray smoke, he leaned against a tree slightly down the road from her house, trying to look harmless and boring in his good suit. He must have done a decent job, he figured, because nobody called the cops. He propped himself in a way that give him a good view of the wide, half-moon driveway, and stood just close enough to see the door through the thick bars of the black steel fence, far enough not to get caught for a Peeping Tom.

It was a hell of a trick, if he did say so himself.

He stayed at his tree for a good couple of hours, pretend-smoking and watching an endless parade of rich Negroes pass by. About two and a half hours passed before Leonie's front door opened.

The entire family spilled out, or, at least, Golden assumed it was the family, laughing and talking from between the open red doors. The father he'd met the other night, a beautiful older woman who was a version of Leonie he could easily get used to, then a younger girl. And in the midst of the chattering family walked Leonie.

At night, with lamplight glowing around her face and figure, she was everything he'd never dared to dream. In the sunlight, her beauty just about dropped him dead.

Golden shoved his hands in his pockets, and if they were trembling he was just going to ignore that fact. How did a woman like this even exist in real life? He crushed out his cigarette and tossed it into a nearby trashcan to join the others from earlier in the morning.

He thanked his lucky stars the family started walking down the drive instead of hopping into an automobile. They didn't go far, only to a church a few minutes away, one with deep and melodious bells ringing the tenth hour by the time they made it up the long walkway. A purposeful stream of other families, including the girls Leonie had gone to Rosie's with that first night, followed them into the church.

They were a social bunch. Instead of going right in to begin their worship, nearly every man, woman, and child milled around the big church yard with other families, chatting and basking in the heat of the late Sunday morning.

Golden stood near them but apart, remembering his mother and the Sunday afternoon rituals she'd loved. Walking down their dirt road to the small Baptist church she and her best friend had gone to since they were children. Making food for the annual church picnic. Getting her weekly sip from the Opal fountain of gossip. For his mother, going to church wasn't so much an expression of faith but a means of seeking out the community she loved and enjoyed being part of.

Sundays were the days you found out who was sleeping with who, who had run off and left their wife or husband, which family was suddenly expecting a little one. They were also the days she didn't have to be "poor Mrs. Worth who'd lost all those babies, and her husband besides." On Sundays, she was just another woman everyone welcomed with open arms. That was what she'd told Golden, at least, when he was hesitant about taking her out during her last days. Those last days, when she needed his help and wasn't able to make it down the dirt road on her own.

That same church had been there when she was dying. Its congregation brought Golden food, seemed ready to catch him if he fell apart. But he was more his daddy's child than his mama's, so he'd buried his pain in his music until it seemed like he hadn't lost anything at all.

The bells of Leonie's church rang and abruptly yanked Golden from the past. His chest ached and the slime of unwanted emotion dripped down his throat. He swallowed thickly and turned back to the group on the porch of the church. Leonie stood there, in her element, angelic in a fluttery blue dress and a wide-brimmed hat shading her face from the morning sun. The sleeves of the dress were long enough to hide the bandage low on her arm.

A man near her own age laughed at something she said, leaning in with his hand indecently close to her behind. Was that the kind of man she really wanted? Good-looking enough. Well-dressed and slender, with no sign of any muscles of hard work showing through the neat drape of his clothes. Leonie laughed again, a flash of those bright teeth against the deep pink lips he'd dreamed of the night before.

Damn. What was he even doing here? Nothing in this place belonged to him.

The urge to see Leonie again had taken him over since he watched her disappear into her house on Saturday night. He wanted to touch her again. He wanted to breathe in her smell. But watching her with the people she belonged with, he realized he *shouldn't* see her again.

She was a bright star and he was just the idiot who'd thought she was just another lightning bug. He knew better now. Every move she made since they met confirmed she was well aware of the power she had. In her own eyes, she was everything. He was nothing.

She'd stopped the madness of her pursuit, but that didn't mean it was his turn to take up the chase. Twisting his lips in self-mockery, Golden turned away. If he hurried, he could grab the next streetcar and ride it back to his neighborhood. The other night, Clive and his girl had invited him to their cookout in the tiny backyard they shared with their neighbors. Golden should stick with the people he knew. He didn't belong anywhere near Leonie.

Halfway down the church path, he thought he heard her call his name.

"Golden. Wait!"

He squeezed his eyes shut. Then, after shoving his hands into his pockets, he turned to face her.

Damn, she was gorgeous.

Seeing her in the daylight from a distance was one thing, but up close? He felt like his mouth had dropped open like the true country bumpkin she thought he was. The pale blue church dress was the color of a clear Georgia sky and skimmed the smooth lines of her body in an ungodly way. The line of buttons down her chest brought his eyes immediately to her breasts, then down to the narrow of her waist, the tempting curve of her hips. Golden squeezed the match safe in his pocket—hard—and forced himself to get back on track.

"Mornin'." He worked hard at a careless grin and tapped the brim of his hat.

"What are you doing here?" she asked once she'd caught up with him, a hand holding on to her hat to stop it from flying away.

She was slightly out of breath, and watching the heaving curve of her breasts did it to him again. Throat dry, arousal uncurling in his lap.

"What, I can't go to church with the good folks in your neighborhood?"

She frowned at him, faint disappointment in her elegant features. "You know that's not what I mean."

Did he? That wasn't important, anyway. He waved away her frown. "I'm up here checking up on a promise."

"Promise? What do you mean?"

"That conversation you wanted to have when we were at my place." Although it hadn't been so much of a conversation as Leonie's continued assault on his virtue. He smirked at the thought. "Let's meet up someplace and talk more."

Her starlight eyes gleamed. She smiled and her dimple flashed at him. "I'd like that."

Church bells rang out suddenly and Golden flinched. In a few minutes, she would be gone.

"How about Wheatley Park?" he suggested. "The statue near the front gates."

"I know it. That's perfect."

"Tuesday?" It was his next day off from the restaurant. "Noon?"

"I'll be there." She raised her voice slightly above the irritating clang of church bells. He wanted to hear her voice, not this damn noise. "I have to go now." Leonie waved her hand behind her, to the church where most of the people had already disappeared inside.

Golden squeezed and released his hand around the match safe in his pocket. He wanted to touch her, but didn't dare. If he started, he probably wouldn't be able to stop. "Okay. Tuesday at noon. Wheatley Park."

"Yes." With a swish of her skirts, she turned to follow the others who belonged in that place, leaving Golden alone in the suddenly silent churchyard.

A brisk wind wormed past the collar of his shirt. The bright morning sun stung the side of his face, his lips. It was like Leonie had touched him and kissed him, leaving him both frozen and burning, still wanting that dangerous fire she both tempted him with and warned him against.

But now, Golden couldn't stay away from her even if he tried.

6

———

Tuesday came quickly. One minute, Golden paced in his room wondering what the hell he had to actually *talk* about with a woman like Leonie, and the next he was walking up to the statue of Phyllis Wheatley, heart knocking in his throat. The bronze likeness of the poet smiled benevolently down at everyone in the park while a gray sky loomed overhead.

Leonie was already waiting.

She sat at the foot of the statue, her back resting on the marble, reading a book.

"You're early," he said, standing over her.

With a tilt of her head, she looked up from her book. Her eyes flickered over his plain dark pants, then up to his shirt and tie, his bare head. Golden hadn't felt like wearing his suit today. Besides, he'd need it tonight for his gig at Rosie's.

"And you're late, at least according to my father's standards." She put a dark blue ribbon between the pages of her book, closed it, then slipped it into her purse. "He says to be early is on time, but to be on time is to be late."

"That doesn't make any sense."

"It works for him," she said. "Especially in his dealings with white people, who always expect Negroes to be late."

Golden didn't bother telling her his grandfather's philosophy. The old man always said he'd never be a slave to the white man's clock. He'd had enough of the other kind of slavery to last him until he was cold in the ground.

"This where you want to sit?" he asked, when she showed no signs of getting to her feet.

"No, not really." She extended a hand to him. "Help me up."

He pulled her up, forgetting about her slight weight and tugging her harder than he needed to. Leonie tumbled into him with a low laugh. The slow and reluctant way she stepped back from him pulled at his lower, dirtier feelings.

That wasn't what he needed right now.

"How's your cut?" He distracted himself with the question, gesturing to the arm she kept covered under the long sleeve of yet another expensive-looking dress. This one was a pale shade of orange.

"It's good." Leonie tugged the sleeve down with a careless shrug and a smile. "This little scratch barely hurts anymore. My parents haven't even noticed it." Her tone said she wasn't sure if that was a good or a bad thing.

"Good. As long as it's not infected, or anything."

"It's completely fine. You took *very* good care of me that night." She licked the corner of her lips and his knees almost buckled.

Jesus. She was driving him to crazy town on the fast train.

Golden bit his tongue hard and willed his arousal not to show. "Where do you want to go?"

Leonie laughed, husky and low. She was merciless. "This is your show, Golden one." She finished teasing him with a flutter of lashes and a squeeze of his arm. "Where do you want to take me?" Leonie slipped the string of her purse over her wrist and tucked her arm around his.

With that obvious end—for now—to her aggressive flirtation, he breathed a quiet sigh of relief and turned his attention to what they'd come here for.

It was a grim day. A canopy of gray had settled overhead, shadowing the afternoon with gloom. No rain, not yet. Golden had half-expected Leonie to cancel, or at least not show up, using the weather as an excuse to back out of seeing him.

Even with his nerves rocketing through him like a low-grade fever, he was glad Leonie came. Wheatley Park was one of his favorites and he wanted to share it with her.

With its wide-branched trees and narrow lanes leading nowhere and everywhere, the park was a beautiful maze. It catered to all types—poor and rich, single and coupled, loud and quiet, Negro and white. It was the perfect place for two people as different as he and Leonie to meet.

In his first days in the city, Golden had spent many hours there. Sometimes, he walked the gardens that ripened in beautiful color for spring; other times, he simply sat and relaxed his weary bones and remembered the good parts of where he came from.

Their footsteps fell in sync on the paved path through the park. The path was one of many leading in a never-ending meander through the woods, beneath the blossoming trees. To Golden, the sweet smell in the air and the open space invited whoever walked there to keep on going, or to simply stop whenever they were ready.

"So, you like this place?"

"Yeah," he said. "It feels good here."

But maybe it wasn't her kind of place. Not fancy enough. No promenade for people to watch her sway by.

"Why do you like it?" she asked. "You don't strike me as a park person, not really."

"What? Do you think I only live and die in a dance hall?" He challenged her with a look, daring her to say what was really on her mind.

Of course, she picked up his challenge with the haughty raise of her eyebrow.

"What I think is that you're a country boy," she said, looking at him like a bug under a magnifying glass. "You like simple things. A drink, your music, maybe even a girl on your lap every once in a while, but none of these things in excess. You have another hunger inside you, for something more." She tapped her chin, like she was thinking hard about what else to say to him. It was obvious, though, that what she wanted was right on the tip of her tongue. "There's something you want even more than these simple things you have. You're moving toward it, even though it's hell on your life right now."

Well, damn.

Like any bug would, he squirmed under her undivided attention. But only on the inside. "You seem to think you know a lot about me for a woman who's seen me only three times."

"And I've been in your apartment, don't forget." Her lashes fluttered and fanned low for a moment, like the distraction of a memory. Then she looked back up at him. "I saw the picture of your mama, your instruments, the big empty space left by things you don't have."

"Like what? A woman like you?"

"Maybe." She shrugged, a slow roll of her shoulders that invited his eyes, his touch. "I know you want me."

She tipped her head to look at him slyly, all silky lashes and tempting mouth, and he couldn't have denied that last part even if he'd been in the habit of making a liar of himself. Golden fingered the silver match holder in his pocket, turned it over and over again. Leonie was as dangerous to him as the blade she carried. Pretty and sharp, with many different ways to cut. Just because the knife in her purse was closed didn't make it any less dangerous.

They kept walking. Her expensive shoes kept pace effortlessly with his worn and old leather boots on the path.

"So, am I right about any of it?" she asked.

His funds. His life. His dreams. All dissected by a woman who didn't give a damn about any of those things.

Golden shrugged. "Right or wrong, I don't know why you're out here with me if those are the things you see. There's not much here for a spoiled girl like you."

"I may be spoiled, but there's more to me than my clothes and my father's house."

"Yeah, like how you came out to light a fire in me just to impress your friends." Those jewel girls were sharp bits of cut glass. As much as he'd like to say that Leonie did not belong among them, she did. She was as glittery and vicious as any of them, her interest a double-edged blade.

Leonie slid her gaze away, but she didn't deny what she'd done.

"We'd been drinking," she said with a dismissive shrug, as if to say debutants getting sloppy drunk and practically jumping into the laps of musicians happened every day. "You know how it is. Looking like you do, I'm sure girls try to get you into bed all the time."

"Just because someone wants something doesn't mean I'll give it to them." He ignored the part about his looks. Compared to her, he was Frankenstein's monster.

"Even if they ask nicely?" She looked up at him through her lashes. She was a woman who never gave up. But it wasn't like she had to go far to wear him down. He was one step away from giving in to her clumsy seduction, no matter how much of a bad idea it was.

"You don't really want me," he said, and wished it wasn't true. "You like the idea of the tease, maybe of something different. What would happen if I just said yes and took you to bed?"

Her eyes flashed even under the gloomy sky. She grinned. "I know we'd both be *very* happy once we got in it."

God in heaven, she was giddy sometimes. And sexy. Golden gave in to a sudden impulse and lightly pinched her side.

She giggled and jerked away from him.

The sound of her laughter, loud and spontaneous, warmed a vulnerable spot in his chest. It should have worried him, but he wanted that glad sound from her again.

"Tell me," he said, moving closer to her. "What's the craziest thing you've ever done?"

"If I don't count coming here with you..." Her eyebrow lifted. "It would be the night my family got invited with Booker T. Washington to the White House—"

"You're shittin' me?"

"—and my mom said we couldn't go."

Golden felt his mouth drop open. He didn't know which revelation shocked him more, the invitation or the refusal. "That can't be true." This girl was even more out of reach than he thought, not just her big house and her expensive clothes, but a family that got invited to the damn White House.

"Of course it is." She shrugged, like it was no big deal that her family had been invited to—and refused—the place the President of the United States lived and ate and screwed his wife. "Mama put her foot down and I threw the biggest tantrum, as if the invitation had been mine to accept or decline." Her pretty lips curved into a smile, like it was a fond memory. A joke. "But Mama held firm and none of us went. As upset as Papa was, he accepted her decision." Leonie tugged his elbow and they started walking again. "The morning after the dinner we did *not* go to, people lost their minds, white and Negro. As if a black man in the White House, eating dinner in a house built by slaves, was a slap to their collective faces."

Even all the way down in his little Georgia town, Golden had heard about it. Most of the white people had been mad enough to spit. Or organize a lynching party to go up north and "remind" Booker T. Washington of his place. Because of their reaction, it was pretty much guaranteed that never again would another Negro sit down to a formal dinner in that very big and very white house.

"After it happened and all the backlash, Papa was so relieved we didn't go. He didn't stop thanking Mama for a whole solid day." Soft laughter spilled from her lips and her midnight sun gaze sparkled at him.

Attracted by her laughter, a couple walking past just about tripped over themselves looking back at her. Leonie's laughter dried and her face fell into cool lines, as if the humor had never been. It was hard to miss how everything shut down with strange eyes on her. But wasn't she used to it by now?

She dipped her head and turned her face away from them, falling back from him even more. She looked awkward and uncomfortable, like a stranger had just seen her buck naked.

Was she ashamed of being seen with him?

"Something wrong?"

She shocked him again when she didn't deny it. "I shouldn't have come here."

"With me?"

"With you, yes."

In his pants pockets, Golden's hands clenched into fists. This was just like the evening outside of Rosie's, only much worse because he had walked right into this. Knowing the type of woman she was and how far from his world she lived, he had invited her out expecting things to be different.

"The trolley isn't far from here," he finally said, after too long of a strained silence. "You can get the next one in about five minutes—" He looked at his cheap pocket watch, "—if you hurry."

"What? That's not what I mean." She shook her head, but her protest sounded like a halfway thing.

"What did you mean, then?"

Her only answer was silence.

People like her never thought they had to explain themselves. Especially not to anyone who didn't belong in their silver and satin-lined world. Anger throbbed behind his cheekbones. "I'm going back downtown," he said. "I'm sure you can find your way back to your silver spoon world from here."

Then he walked away.

It took everything in him not to go back and escort Leonie back to her part of town. His mama raised him not to be the man stomping his way across a park with hurt feelings, but it was daylight and Leonie didn't want anyone to see them together.

Fuck it.

His hand clenched around the piece of silver in his pocket and flinched, felt it break through the skin, dig in. But Leonie had dug into him much deeper, and it hurt much, much more.

7

Golden picked up his guitar and strummed a few notes. The half-hearted music, slow and maudlin, throbbed like a sickly heartbeat in his one-room apartment.

Pathetic. When he'd escaped Wheatley Park and Leonie's scorn, he thought he needed the company of his friends at Rosie's to make him feel better. But less than an hour in, he was done. Home seemed the logical place to be, but being in the apartment wasn't doing him any favors, either.

In the single chair in the room, he sat with his guitar balanced on his thigh and tried a little harder, plucked the cords to the tune playing in his head, an idea he had for the next time Clive wanted to break into something new.

But the idea that had seemed fresh and hot to him a day before now wasn't. He plucked and hummed, hoping something good would come back to him, but Leonie whipped through his consciousness like a high-wind hurricane, blowing down everything else in her wake. The music. His concentration. Every. Single. Thing.

Damn her.

Golden jumped up from his chair and dropped the guitar before he did something stupid like smash it to pieces. He needed to go out.

It was a bad idea to come back here so soon after seeing her. Practically snarling under his breath, he grabbed his jacket and keys and yanked open the door. He stopped.

Leonie stood in front of him, a hand lifted to knock.

"Hey." Some emotion roughed up her voice. Her eyes flitted over his face, searching.

No. He wasn't going to be fooled again by a cool look and the desire written in every line of her body. That could have been for any man. He was through with all of it.

"What do you want?" he demanded.

"I want you." With a quick breath, she stepped past the threshold of the place he lived, and kissed him.

8

____

Golden was a sharp and brilliant light illuminating all of Leonie's deepest desires. Fierce and hot and burning and Golden. His mouth made her shiver all over.

Oh, God.... He tasted so good.

It had taken every ounce of courage she had to go back to his place and confront him with the words burning on her tongue. She wanted him, but she was afraid. She needed to touch him, but she was terrified of the new desire, uncontrollable and unfamiliar, that clawed at her from the inside when he was on her mind.

From the first time she saw him, the affair was meant to be a lark. Nothing but play to keep her friends amused while they'd been drinking and were desperate to keep the party going. Yes, she'd thought he was beautiful up there on the stage, with sweat making his gilt skin glow like a god's. Yes, she thought she'd seen something in his eyes, a lightning bolt of want that made her bold enough to proposition him.

But as soon as she was close to him, his amber eyes moving over her like she was something special, she wanted to *be* that. She wanted to be a girl a man like him found valuable, incomparable, desirable. But she'd messed it up with her playacting and nearly lost him.

Just like she'd messed it up in the park, when a girl she'd recognized from school looked at her with shock and scorn, making her feel self-conscious, stupid for thinking she could have Golden like a normal woman could have a man. Her parents had tied her to a path from which she had no hope of veering.

Under the girl's stare, Leonie had felt naked, her desire and want for Golden like a stink on her skin everyone could smell. She'd pushed Golden away. Then he'd pushed back, and she hadn't known what to do.

Except this.

"Golden..." His hair was thick under her fingers, strong and rough and beautiful like the man himself. She clung to him, afraid he would push her away and tell her to leave and never come back.

"Do you know what you're doing?" His words were muffled against her mouth but she heard them clear enough.

"You, if we're both lucky." She rubbed against him, dragged her tender breasts over his chest, pressed kisses to the sides of his mouth and down his neck. She had to let him know how much she wanted him. Sensation and desire skittered down her spine.

He grunted, stumbling back, and she felt a pulse of triumph when his hands dug into her waist and pulled her all the way into his room. The door slammed behind them. His jacket and keys fell, then she tumbled to the bed, his heavy body blanketing hers.

"You don't know what you want," he whispered.

With a shudder that wracked his entire body, he kissed her back, hot and hard. Panting, Golden sucked on her tongue, and each pull of his mouth tugged arousal between her thighs. She squirmed against him, shamelessly wet and begging.

Would he give her what she wanted? Would he make love to her like they both needed? She craved his touch. She craved so much of him. Not just his body, but the intelligence burning through his eyes, the adoration lighting him up every time he looked at her.

Did he even know how he looked at her? Did he know she wanted to be everything he saw, and more?

Gasping, she tugged at his shirt, desperate to feel his hot and soft skin stretched over hard muscles and his fiercely pounding heart. She'd held herself back for so long, it felt good to finally let go.

"Careful, girl. This is my only good shirt."

Her senses whirled away completely when he sucked on her throat, hands working the buttons at the back of her dress. She groaned, her body on fire for him. "I'll buy you a new one."

Through a haze of lust, she felt him jerk hard against her, a rejection. She'd said something very wrong, she could feel it in the sudden space between them. But he was finally here, finally touching her skin, finally about to be hers. She couldn't think, only feel.

He put a firm but gentle hand on her throat, keeping her from twisting up and kissing him again. "Are you the one fucking me, or am I fucking you?"

What was he talking about? She squirmed and reached back to undo the buttons herself. Why did he stop?

"Touch me! Damn you, just—" Her words fell away when he did just that. And more.

Golden wrenched her head back with a desperate grip on her hair. He tongued her throat, bit her, sent sparks of want shooting between her legs.

He was panting and sweating, his big body hovering over hers, hot through all their clothes. Too many clothes.

"God...sometimes, I think you don't know half the things you say." With a tortured sound, he flipped her over to her stomach. Was he going to—?

Pleasure winged through her with the touch of his hands on her thighs, dragging up the hem of her dress, baring her thighs and bottom to his gaze. Hot breath huffed against the back of her neck and she shivered, wanted. Begged.

"Golden..." She could only say his name.

Everything she knew had been blown away by the fierceness of her want for him. Her body was passionate, completely alive for the first time. For once, sex was more than just a way to pass the time or prove how modern and powerful she was. She should have waited for this. To feel this fire. To know a man who wanted her this much.

Another whimper left her throat when his hands moved along her back, a swift unbuttoning of her dress, the voluminous fabric pulled down and discarded, her petticoats yanked away and shoved to the floor.

He touched her naked skin, and she nearly exploded. The pressure between her legs became unbearable. Want coiled low and tight in her belly. If he didn't touch her sex now, she would die.

She begged him. She panted. "Please...please!"

Desperate for him, she lifted her bottom for him, expecting him to part her feminine flesh and slip inside, just like her other lovers had done.

But with a firm hand in the center of her back, he only pushed her back down into the sheets. She groaned again when the button of her pleasure ground into the rough bedding and sent sparks of desire shooting through her veins.

"Not like this, baby." He kissed the back of her neck softly, sweetly.

She stilled. Then she shuddered at the long stroke of his tongue down the entire writhing length of her back. He peppered delicate bites along her spine and she sizzled from the outside in.

Leonie was on fire. Burning. Her familiar house razed to the ground, and a new edifice of pleasure slowly erected in its place with each touch of his hands. His mouth, hot and inciting, drifted over the swell of her bottom.

"What are you—oh!"

His teeth sank into her skin. She screamed, a hot cry of sound that echoed in the little room.

"God, you're sweet!"

His hands were on the swell of her hips, then her bottom. He pulled her hips up to force her to kneel in the bed. Another scream rocked through her throat when his mouth touched her, lapping her up from behind. Her hand flailed backward to touch him, to hold on to something while he used his mouth to tear her world apart.

"Please, please, please—" She didn't know what she was begging for, but she wanted it, needed it.

Light and heat scoured through her until she barely knew her own name. She only knew that Golden was finally touching her and changing everything she ever knew about sex, about lovemaking, about the things a man could make a woman feel.

The sound of him pleasing her—liquid laps of his tongue on her quim, groaning sighs like he was enjoying taking her apart, his deep and growling voice. All these things turned her on as much as the flick of his tongue on the pearl controlling her pleasure. Golden was ruthless. A rough suck, fingers like a hummingbird, his vibrating moans on her most intimate of spaces. Her climax rammed toward her and tumbled her, shuddering, all the way down into the sheets.

She was well and done.

Her body flopped down, shuddering, into the bed. She didn't protest when Golden turned her onto her back. Swimming in the remnants of her satisfaction, she knew how she must have looked to him. Undone. Loose and well-pleasured.

"I could get used to seeing you like this, lioness."

His damp mouth, scented with her body, dipped down to hers and licked the taste of her own quim into her, a decadent and wet flavor. She swallowed it with a helpless moan.

So. Good.

Satisfied as she was, the rough scrape of Golden's clothes all over her naked body spurred her again, and she opened her legs, wrapping them around him and pushing her hips up into his while they kissed. The slick sound of their mouths moving together twisted lust around her even more tightly.

His mouth moved down her neck in long, sucking kisses. Golden took his time with her, biting her neck, puffing his hot breath against her sensitive skin. She felt him, firm and hot against her thighs. He must have been desperate to have her, but he made no move to unbutton himself.

"Golden, take me," she moaned. He squeezed her breast and she reached for the front of his trousers, hands fumbling.

But he pulled back from her, and she whimpered with the loss.

"No!" Her hands clawed into him, but he took himself away from her anyway, sitting back on his knees in the bed.

"Don't move, my lioness." His voice was rough with want, but he was in perfect control.

Carefully, he took off his tie, unbuttoned his shirt and pulled it from his slacks, revealing in no great hurry the hard planes of his chest, dark brown nipples, a belly rippling with muscle. Those gorgeous muscles flexed when he pulled the shirt from his slacks. He shrugged it off, then leaned over to one side to put it on the very nearby chair.

He was torturing her.

Leonie groaned and bit her lip. Two could play that game.

While he watched, she put a hand between her legs, touching herself, teasing open the petals of her desire. She heard him catch his breath, and swore the thick length of him under the fabric of his trousers twitched toward her.

"While you're taking your sweet time, you could be here." She opened her legs wide to show him what he as missing.

Eyes going a darker gold, he groaned. His shoes clattered to the floor. His socks followed, then his trousers. It didn't happen as fast as she would have liked, but it was fast enough. She got only the barest glimpse of him—slim hips, thick sex rising from its unexpectedly red-tinged nest, leaking and hard and nudging the laddering packs of muscle on his belly—before he fell on top of her.

"Oh!" A grunt of air left her body with the abrupt fall of his weight. A giggle rose up from her throat. "You're heavier than you look."

"You like to tease?" His voice rumbled, the control in it gone. He shoved between her thighs, and she laughed again and hooked her legs around his hips, inviting him in. But even in the midst of his desperation, he didn't just *take*. He knew she was ready. He knew she'd already gotten her satisfaction.

"You want this?" He lined himself up without waiting for an answer, allowed her to feel the thick head of him just barely nudging into her. She bit her lip at the sting of pleasure, the slow opening of the entrance of her most delicate place.

"Yes..." And she tilted her hips up and swallowed him completely.

They both groaned, long and low. The rumble of sound shook her to her very core, and she tightened instinctively around him.

God, so good.

Trembling, he cursed at her ear and panted, his hardness buried deep inside her, his body firm and hot and still. Leonie curled her hips up to receive him more deeply.

"Lioness, I think you're trying to kill me."

The fire shivered through her. She *was* going to kill him if he didn't move. She squeezed him again, her internal muscles working him hard while he stayed motionless inside her. He groaned, breath puffing hard in her throat.

She twisted her hips under him, desperate for him to move, hunting for her own pleasure and forcing his out of hiding.

He cursed again. "If you—God damn...if you don't stop...this will be over before either of us wants it to be."

"We have to at least start," she gasped, moving her hips and rubbing her aching nipples against his broad chest.

"Okay, lioness." He gripped her hips to hold her in one place, levered himself up on his arms to look into her eyes. The golden orbs burned down into her, the desire in them humbling and fierce. His hips moved, a slow and grinding motion that ramped up her breath.

Gasping, she threw her head back and latched her nails into the shifting muscles of his hard shoulders. Pleasure pooled in her belly like honey, dripping its sweetness down her body, slicking wet around him, trickling between her thighs.

"Golden, please...oh, please..."

He began a pulse-pounding rhythm, slow, then fast, then slow again, a questing knock at the door of her pleasure. Leonie unraveled.

Her hips rose up to meet his again, and again. They slapped together. Groaned together. Sweat ran slick between their bodies. Their cries of pleasure stroked Leonie's ears and the heart of her lust.

Faster.

Harder.

His grunts were primal now. His grip on her hips relentless. The slap of skin against skin added to the impending crescendo of the most magnificent performance she'd ever been a part of.

She cried out his name while the pleasure buzzed and fizzed and rolled and wrecked her. Her sex clutched desperately at his hardness.

The orgasm crashed into her. Unexpected, devastating. Leonie screamed again and arched her body in the sheets, circling her hips. Even in the midst of her pleasure's crisis, she clasped wetly at him, desperate to tug him over the edge with her.

Then it happened. His lust reached its peak in a shocked shout of pleasure that left her ears ringing.

They lay together, panting and sweating, gasping each other's air until, finally, he rolled off her and onto his back.

Leonie stared up at the ceiling, her breath still puffing hard in the otherwise quiet room. The sheets rustled as he moved next to her.

"I hope your chase was worth it," he said with a pleased gleam in his Midas eyes. Of course, he knew he'd upended her world. How could he not?

She licked her dry lips to get some moisture back into them and shoved damp hair back from her face. Her heart was knocking loud enough in her chest to thud in her ears like war drums. She swallowed a panting breath.

She turned to look at him, amazement still in her eyes. "Oh, it was all right."

His laughter rolled through the room like music.

9

Because it was so good, and *he* was so good, they made love again less than an hour later. This time, she was on top, his hard body at her mercy and completely under her control. At the end, she felt as if she'd been broken and put back together again.

She lay on her side and watched him, the flickering of his lashes as he blinked his breath back, the heaving dampness of his chest. The emotion that had driven her to his door—lust, peppered with a heavy dose of fascination—rose up in her again.

He was so very vital, so beautiful, that he seemed like a prince from another world. She knew so little about him: that he loved his music, that he knew himself enough to turn away from her tricks and foolishness, that he was as fierce and perfect in bed as he was on stage. She knew these things, but she wanted to know so much more. Maybe even everything.

"Seems like you're thinking about a lot over there." Golden eyes gently pinned her where she lay.

A blush burned her cheeks. "What's there for me to think about after your thorough handling? I can barely remember my name, much less string any thoughts together." No way was she ready to confess her near obsession with who he was, and not just for how well he made her cum.

Leonie sat up and stretched, smiling as his gaze devoured her nakedness. Those looks of his were addictive. Because of that alone, she couldn't afford to stay around him too much longer.

Her body shamelessly bare, she climbed from the bed and pulled on her white drawers and thin cotton chemise. "Where's your bathroom?"

Still lounging against the pillows, he jerked his chin toward the door. "To the left and down the hall."

She couldn't hide her surprise. Vaguely, she remembered him leaving the room the night she'd been attacked and coming back with a wet cloth and bowl of water. She never imagined he'd have to leave his own rooms to use the toilet. Or bath.

Fine, she could do this. It wasn't like this could become a regular practice. Leonie nodded once. On her way out, she grabbed one of the folded hand towels she saw by the door, along with a bar of soap from its small boat-shaped dish.

After tending to herself, she returned to find him sitting in the room's only chair. He was naked except for the sheet wrapped around his waist and a guitar in his lap.

He lightly strummed the guitar with long fingers while she watched. The melody of an almost-song bounced between the walls of the small room. And the room *was* small, only a quarter the size of her own bedroom and darkly lit, lamps glowing above the bed and on top of the ratty-looking dresser. He must have put matches to the lamps while she was in the bathroom.

Leonie put the soap away and hung the cleaned rag she'd used on a rack by the door. "Thank you," she said.

He looked at her with a wry twist of his mouth. "You're welcome, even though I didn't actually offer."

"You would have if you'd thought about it," she teased, and climbed back into bed.

The remaining thin sheet, stretched over the mattress, smelled like them. His sweat and her perfume. The elixir of their sex.

From the chair, he watched her with considering eyes, maybe trying to figure out exactly what she was. Maybe even trying to scheme ways to get her to be his. Leonie scoffed silently. She burned with a reluctant want for him, but she was no one's to take. She didn't even belong to herself.

"You know, I wouldn't mind getting some of that wet cloth to clean myself up with," Golden said.

He strummed the guitar while his eyes remained light as silk on her face, making the comment seem idle in the extreme. After all, he had himself all covered up with the sheet, and had probably wiped up with it as well. He seemed happy enough to marinate in the results of their night's work.

Leonie leaned back in the bed and watched his hands. "Then you should have told me before I left." She was considerate enough and would have done it if he asked. Never mind this had never been something any of her other lovers had asked of her before.

"And now?" A playful song tripped from the guitar in his lap, something vaguely familiar she could not name. It reminded her of spring.

She shrugged and didn't move.

His guitar strummed on about spring and he laughed, a soft sound with only a touch of scorn. "You're spoiled."

"I just don't want to move. Is that so bad? I mean, you'd probably feel the same if you were in my shoes." Then she looked down at her bare feet with a smile. "Well, my chemise."

But she couldn't stop staring at him for long. Sitting there, with his country boy's guitar, he should have been a silly cliché. The breadth of his sweat-damp chest, the sheets gathered low in his lap to show off the muscular ridges of his belly and the fine trail of hair leading to his sex, his blazing amber eyes. All these things made the entire picture of him too erotic to be anywhere near funny.

"You're wrong, though," he said. "I'd get up and bring the whole bathroom to you right now if you want it."

His words sent warmth to her chest and a zing of electricity straight to her quim. She squirmed on the bed, suddenly uncomfortable. Her fingers curled into the sheet on either side of her hips, desperately grabbing for an anchor to prevent herself from climbing into his lap and pressing kisses all over him like some infatuated harem girl.

"You're entirely too generous for your own good. I've heard that about you Southern boys. You can take the boy out of the country...." She raised a suggestive eyebrow at him.

He said nothing else for a moment, only played his guitar, strumming notes to what was obviously a country song while giving her another teasing smile. His eyes glimmered like the most precious of stones.

"You know, I'm working on something now," he said. "It's something to take me out of Rosie's and Joe's restaurant downstairs and over to Europe someplace."

She shrugged and mentally shifted with his sudden change in topic. His lack of response to the barbs she threw out put more distance between them. It was troubling in ways she didn't want to consider. "That's good, right?"

"It's real good. Rosie's place gets me in front of more people who like my music, but I've been here long enough to want more." His fingers paused over the guitar strings. "And I usually get what I want."

A delicious shiver worked its way up her spine. "It must be nice."

"Yeah, but not for the sake of just having something." The guitar hummed on and Golden's accent thickened on the last of his words. The drunkening moonshine and clover honey in his voice poured into her ear, sweet and addictive. "I want to be content, that's all. I want a woman to call my own, enough money to put a roof over our heads, maybe take her out once in a while and buy her pretty trinkets. Simple things. Nothing like pearls or diamonds, or any of that stuff." He winced then, a shadow moving across his face as if he'd just remembered something.

"Most men have all that," Leonie said. "So it should be simple enough for you to get, too." But why was he telling her this? His imagined future had nothing to do with her.

He laughed. "God, you're so naïve about things outside of your little mini palace on top of the world."

She refused to rise to the bait. Of course, she'd had it easy, especially compared to other Negroes in America. She knew that all too well, so she wasn't going to argue with him about it.

Instead, she focused on what his words really meant. What would it be like to have such simple dreams and desires? A vision for the future that was hers, not just a future someone else thought she should have? She tried to imagine wanting these things: a man of her own and enough money to keep both of them sheltered and eating well enough. Money enough to cultivate a simple kind of joy.

Leonie couldn't imagine it at all.

Maybe that was her problem. Her mother always said she had a lack of imagination.

"What about you?" Golden strummed. This time, the music was a bit more sensual, an unfamiliar rhythm Leonie's body took notice of. Loose and rested, she unconsciously swayed to the music.

"What kind of happiness are you looking for?" he asked.

"Happiness is for fools, you know that?" She swayed in his bed and watched him, feeling her eyelids fall low and heavy. Was he hypnotizing her with his damn guitar? Was she allowing it?

"Then be a fool with me...." He hummed a vague tune then, abruptly stopped playing and set the guitar aside. "What would you like, my lioness?"

I'm not your anything. But the words wouldn't come. "I'd like to be my own person," she said instead.

She tipped her head back and closed her eyes. The music still flowed through her, put there by the sneaky bastard just like he'd slipped his penis into her and opened her to ridiculous possibilities. Ones that didn't even make sense.

The obligation her mother hung over her was unshakable. A powerful and beloved mother to disappoint; a brother whose memory she would spit on. No, happiness was not so easy to achieve.

She drew a deep breath in through her nose and brought her head back up.

"But it's not so simple." Her heart thumped just hard enough to hurt when she thought again of what she wanted in order to be happy, and what others wanted for her. Leonie breathed out the discomfort, breathed in strength, and pulled herself together. "Listen, I've got to go."

She got up from the bed and pulled on her clothes. Golden, his sheet forgotten in a puddle by the chair, was there to button the back of her dress once she pulled the fabric over her arms and up to her throat.

"You can stay the night here, if you want." Naked, he stepped back once he finished fastening all the buttons he'd undone just a couple of hours before.

Leonie bit her lip and looked away from the tempting sight of his beautiful body, firmly muscled and unashamed in the soft light flickering from the lamps in the small room. God. her palms itched to touch him again. The space between her legs, where she'd cleaned so well before, became slippery once again. Nerves and unwelcome desire brought her tongue across her dry lips.

"Thank you, but I can't," she said, looking anywhere but at him. "My parents will worry."

Before Leonie left her house, she'd stuffed pillows under her blanket to make it seem like she was still in bed. Because of that, she figured she should be fine for most of the night, but if she didn't come down for their early breakfast, the entire household would go crazy. She'd asked her sister to cover for her, but Anna could only do so much.

Then her father would call his friend in the police commissioner's office to put together a search party for Leonie, or something equally ridiculous. Leonie didn't want that humiliation. Or the disappointment sure to be in her mother's eyes.

"I guess I'd worry myself dumb if I had a daughter like you wandering around town," he said.

Behind her, she heard the rustle of fabric and hoped Golden was putting some clothes on.

Why the sight of his naked body flustered her, when she'd

ridden him to paradise and back barely an hour ago, was a complete mystery to her. The memory of it froze her where she stood: the slick rasp of pubic hair on pubic hair, the grimace of agonized pleasure on his face when he came, the pulse after pulse of blessed release that left her weak and nearly sobbing beneath him.

Face burning, Leonie turned away to find her purse. When she found it under his bed—along with her shoes—she climbed up from her knees to see him fully dressed.

"Where—?"

"If you think I'm going to watch you walk out of here and not see you to your front door, you're crazier than you act." His smile took any sting out of the words. He shoved his keys in his pockets, waving her toward the door. "Let's get going. It's getting late."

They made it across town on the streetcar with few words between them. Leonie felt exhausted from the sex, tired from over-thinking, and uneasy about what was happening between them.

But there wasn't anything going on. He was a nice boy with a beautiful penis. She was a rich girl with a bright future: she was about to go to Radcliffe College to fulfill her parents' dreams. Leonie rolled her eyes at herself. If only it was so clear and simple.

At her house, Golden waited until she was inside her front door to walk away. Perched behind the slit of a curtain inside the darkened house, she watched him. His rolling and slightly bow-legged walk. The glint of the streetlight on his not-quite-black hair.

Idiot. What the hell are you doing?

Only when he was gone, disappeared around the corner and down the street toward the streetcar stop, did she tiptoe upstairs to her bedroom. Standing in the dark, she debated whether or not to take a shower. The pillows shaped into a body under the blankets were just where she'd left them. She was still contemplating a shower when her door squeaked open. She jumped back into the shadows with a silent gasp.

Did her mother figure everything out?

"Leonie?" Her sister's whisper sounded faintly in the room. "I know you're back. I heard you on the stairs." Holding a small candle, Anna closed the door behind her and came in.

Damn.

Resigned to her sister's nosiness, Leonie crept out from behind the curtain and began removing the pillows from under the blanket.

"What do you want, Anna? I'm tired."

Her sister, all of fifteen but with the curiosity of a ninety-year-old grandmother, sat on the edge of the bed and smirked. Her tiny teeth glinted in the candlelight. "I bet you are, Leonie. Are you going to tell me who you were with?"

Before she left, Leonie asked her sister to cover for her without telling her why. Leonie hadn't planned on sleeping with Golden, or at least she hadn't counted on it really happening. After he'd pushed her away so many times, she was half-convinced she'd been wasting her time. Never had she been so glad to be wrong.

She fluffed the extra pillows and put them back in their rightful place at the top of the bed. Then she turned the covers down and twitched the sheets up the way she liked them. Once she ran out of meaningless distractions, she crossed her arms over her chest and glared at Anna.

"It's no one you know," she said finally.

That was true enough. Anna hadn't gone along with Leonie that night to the bar. Younger by seven years, Anna was too young to do most things that were interesting to Leonie, but their bond as sisters was unshakeable. They shared secrets, joys, and heartaches. Everything else, Leonie experienced with Dawn and Verna. Leonie and the two girls had grown up together, put off going to college together, and would finally enter Radcliffe in the fall. Together.

When Leonie had left with them for Rosie's, she only planned on drinking, maybe finding a boy or three to flirt with. What happened instead with Golden shocked her, but it made her a little glad. If it wasn't for her girls, she wouldn't have met him.

"You don't know who I know," Anna pouted, once the silence continued past her liking.

"I actually do, Anna Evangeline Harper."

Even in the dark, she saw her sister roll her eyes. "Fine." With the candle on the bedside table, Anna crossed her arms, a mirror of Leonie's pose. "Are you going to tell me, or what?"

Leonie hesitated. Anna had covered for her, this time. But she also kept secrets like spread fingers held water. Within a day or two, she'd tell her gossiping little friends all about Leonie's night out, and before Leonie knew it, they'd all know she'd fallen into bed with a country boy guitar player who made it hard for her to think straight.

"I won't tell you his name, but I'll tell you I won't be seeing him again. School—" Could she trust Anna with more? "—school's just around the corner, and he's not the kind of guy Mama would approve of."

"That's no information at all!" Anna hissed in a fierce whisper. "You might as well tell me you were making time with an imaginary friend. Not fair!"

"Anna!"

"You..." Her sister trailed off in a sputter.

Leonie was very certain an insult waited for her on Anna's bitter tongue. A hand on her hips, she wagged a finger in her sister's face. "You know you're a tattletale, at least to your friends. I can't let you know any more about him."

"Even after I kept Mama and Papa off your back tonight?"

"I'm sorry." And Leonie was. Anything else, she'd trust her sister with, but not this. Their circles were too small, and it would probably take the nosiest of her friends only about ten seconds to find out who Golden was. And then, even her parents would find out.

Anna jumped to her feet in a huff. She grabbed her candle and the flame stuttered with her furious movements. "All right, Leonie. Have it your way." She flounced to the door, then spun back to face Leonie so fast her candle blew furiously and nearly went out. "By the way, you stink. You should wash that man off you before you push it in Mama and Papa's faces in the morning." She yanked the door open and dashed down the hall.

Damn it.

Leonie groaned and closed the door after her sister, then sniffed herself. Did she still smell like what she and Golden had done? She sniffed again and only smelled day-old perfume along with the faintest hint of sweat. His sweat?

The thought of it made Leonie warm all over.

I must be losing my mind.

But, God, what a way to lose it.

10

———

"Good morning, Mama. Papa."

Leonie sashayed into breakfast as if nothing out of the ordinary happened the night before. No Golden. No sneaking in past the household's bedtime. Certainly no dreams of sex and desire that left her breathless and damp between her thighs. The bath she took had been extra hot, and extra long.

The curtains were wide-open, letting in the brilliant morning sun. The smell of coffee, bacon, and maple syrup sweetened the room. Her father looked up from his morning paper, for the moment ignoring the massive breakfast—eggs, bacon, waffles, toast—in front of him. "Good morning, Leonie." His voice was low, but it carried through the large dining room, an effective weapon when he was in court.

Seated next to him, her mother lifted her coffee cup for the hovering maid, Carlotta, to refill. "Don't you look bright and cheerful this morning," she said. Her skin, like the desert at high noon, glowed against her emerald day dress.

Footsteps sounded on the tiles behind Leonie. Anna came in, quickly tying the ribbon at her waist. Her sister stuck out her tongue and made a point of sitting on the opposite side of the table from Leonie instead of right next to her, like she normally did.

Brat.

Her father rattled his paper and folded it beside his place, ready to eat now that the whole family was down for breakfast. "What's going on with you two this morning?"

Of course, he would notice.

"Nothing, Papa," Leonie said. "Anna is just being silly." She dropped a light kiss on his weathered cheek and smiled automatically when his whiskers tickled her lips. She took her own chair just as Carlotta slid a plate in front of her. Unlike her father's, hers only contained a slice of cantaloupe, scrambled eggs, and two triangles of toast. Despite her long night, she felt energized and ready to conquer the day.

"You didn't answer me, dear," her mother said. "What's got you smiling from ear to ear? Normally, it would be too early for you to even wish your father and me a proper good morning." A slight exaggeration, but Helen Harper was prone to those. "You look positively giddy."

True, Leonie wasn't usually a morning person but she was certain there nothing *giddy* about the way she was acting. "Nothing, Mama. It's just a nice morning. The sun is shining. We're alive. The usual."

Her mother made a disbelieving sound. Her sister snorted.

"Do *you* know something, Anna?" Despite her mother's insistent questioning, she didn't seem all that interested in the answer. As a tireless suffragette also working toward true equality for Negroes in this country, she was often busy from morning until late afternoon. She saw breakfast as the time to catch up with her family before she got back to the things she was truly concerned about.

"Not at all, Mama," Anna said with an unconvincing shrug. "Leonie doesn't tell me a thing."

Leonie rolled her eyes. But she wanted to hug her sister for not volunteering anything that would make breakfast awkward. With a quick grin at Anna, she picked up her fork and began to eat. Utensils clattered against plates, and the room filled the usual dining sounds

—requests for salt and pepper, appreciative grunts, Anna's chatter about what she was into at school with her friends.

"I heard from the Scotts today." Her mother waved a letter she picked up from beside her plate. "Alberta is planning on going someplace down South to teach soon."

Leonie looked up. The Scotts were friends of her mothers who lived in Cambridge and whose daughter, Alberta, was the first Negro ever to graduate from Radcliffe College. The women loved each other, but they'd also carried a healthy rivalry ever since they were young.

"That dangerous place?" her father asked with one of his famous frowns. "I hear they're hanging Negroes from trees left and right down there." He thought the entire South was the same. To be fair, the entire family did.

"Exactly. I heard the same thing. Just last week, some friends of mine in the Negro Justice Coalition were warning people, no matter how light the skin, not to set a single foot down there." Her mother shuddered theatrically.

The South. Golden was from someplace down there. An image of him hanging from one of those magnolia trees crawled into Leonie's imagination and she dropped her fork on the plate with a clatter.

"But," Helen Harper continued, her tone filled with doubt "—from what her mother says, Booker T. Washington himself recruited her to work down there at his institute." She obviously didn't believe a word of it. It was no matter that the Scotts and her parents moved in similar circles; her father was the one who knew Mr. Washington and had been invited to join him in various endeavors. "You know, Leonie," her mother said. "If you had had any interest in teaching, I'm sure you would have been the one invited down there."

But she didn't want to teach. She certainly didn't want to be the pawn in her mother's game to outdo her Cambridge friends. All she wanted to do was live her own life.

Leonie shoved the fruit around on her plate. She couldn't eat another bite.

"Alberta already graduated from college, Mama," Anna said.

At the same time, her father rapped his knuckles on the table. It was a light noise, but it commanded everyone's attention. "No child of mine is going to a place where they lynch Negroes, no matter who issues the invitation." Her father liked Mr. Washington enough, but he did disagree with some of his beliefs.

"It's quite an honor to be asked, though," her mother said, ignoring the gentle warning in her husband's voice. "This is not like that unwise business with the White House invitation. This would lead to more opportunities for Leonie. Maybe even for the family. Radcliffe College is the key."

That damn school again. Leonie had already lost her appetite when her father mentioned lynching and the South. With each word her mother spoke, she wanted to jump up from the table, or at least plug her ears like a child.

She cleared her throat. "What if I didn't go to Radcliffe, Mama?"

Everything at the table seemed to stop. Leonie knew it was just her imagination, because her father kept on eating his breakfast and answering Anna's endless questions, but it was her mother's stark look that she saw, the disbelief draining all the softness from her features.

"What do you mean?" The glance her mother leveled at her— eyebrow arched, her body leaning close while her eyes snapped— was clear. *Why on earth would you not go to Radcliffe?*

Her heart knocked hard and fast, but Leonie pushed on, Sisyphus rolling up that impossible boulder. "What if I didn't end up going to Radcliffe? I mean, things could happen." She nibbled at her dry-as-ashes toast and tried for a casual expression.

Her mother put down her knife and fork. "That doesn't make any sense, Leonie. You've been accepted. You matriculate in the fall. It's later than I'd like, but at least you're still going."

At twenty-two, Leonie was the age most girls were leaving undergraduate school and heading to get another degree, get married, or find a job with the potential to end up somewhere remarkable. Like Mr. Washington's Tuskegee Institute.

Leonie dug her fork into the slice of cantaloupe on her plate and cut it into two, then three, pieces. "Plans change all the time, Mama. I mean, what if the school decides to take back their invitation?"

"These plans won't change." Her mother's voice was as hard as the diamonds in her wedding ring. "You're not the first Negro girl to be admitted—" She actually looked pained as she said it, "—so they won't have any issue integrating you into the classrooms or getting you acclimated to their ways."

What about what I want? Leonie wanted to ask. *What if my plans change?* She wanted to whine and protest even more, but that was the end to her boldness. Challenging her mother wasn't something she did regularly, or at all. It was an exhausting and losing battle.

"It's okay, Mama," she said, biting back a sigh. "I was just speaking hypothetically."

Rivalry aside, the death of Leonie's brother, Wallace, had put the burden of success squarely on her shoulders. In a perverted version of having "an heir, a spare, and a mare," with Wallace's death, Leonie had inherited her parents' expectations and the responsibilities of the first-born. Succeed. Make the family proud. Don't make stupid choices that would reflect badly on the family.

It wasn't as if Leonie didn't understand. She did.

Her mother wanted what was best. For all of them. Just like when she'd forbidden her husband from taking them to the White House for dinner last fall, because she'd known the backlash that would come from it. White people and some black people still cursed Mr. Washington's name, to this day, for having had dinner with President Roosevelt. Always, Helen Harper looked out for her family's best interests, even if the "best" hurt in the moment.

Leonie pressed her lips shut.

The breakfast continued on, with her parents talking about Alberta and her bright future, Anna chiming in with her thoughts on the matter. Leonie had never felt so grateful as when Carlotta slipped into the dining room to announce Leonie had guests.

She wiped her lips and stood up. "May I be excused?"

Leonie's father waved his hand toward the sound of female laughter and light conversation in the foyer. "Of course."

"Which of your friends is rude enough to pay a call at breakfast time?" her mother snapped.

"It's probably Verna and Dawn. We're going into the city to buy dresses for the first day at Radcliffe. A store Verna likes is having an early preview sale." It was a blatant lie, but Leonie couldn't think of any other excuse her mother would accept. Any errand toward the start of her Radcliffe matriculation would get instantly approved.

"Oh." Her mother's face cleared. "Go ahead. But I want to see your purchase when you return."

"Of course, Mama." She pressed a dry kiss to her mother's cheek and then did the same to her father. "See you later, Papa."

He looked away from his conversation with Anna, eyes crinkling with humor. "Enjoy your escape, my Leonie." Although her mother was the smartest one in the house, he was a hard one to fool. He didn't become one of the best lawyers in Washington just because of his good looks.

She blew him a smiling kiss and sailed from the room. A few minutes later, Leonie slipped her cloth purse over her wrist and stepped out onto the porch with her two friends.

Verna—generally agreed to be the prettiest of them all with her coal black skin, dark gray eyes, and waist-length curls—looped her arm through Leonie's. "We heard your mother when we walked in. She didn't sound happy at all."

While Verna was gorgeous—she had the kind of beauty that made people stop in the streets and stare—there was also something slightly unsettling about how the mixture of black and white had settled into her features. Her dark skin was lush and powdery, soft to the touch, and it instantly made people want to reach out and see if it was as soft as if looked. Dark girls weren't supposed to be pretty. That was a never-ending mantra Leonie and her friends had heard their entire lives.

But the white boys fell over themselves to get Verna into bed while the black boys and men in their circles constantly propositioned her, naturally only in the politest of ways. Of the three girls in their group, she was the one people always noticed first. Sometimes

Leonie saw people looking at her friend in admiration and sheer lust, the look on their faces saying plainly they didn't know why they were so drawn to her.

When Leonie told Verna this, her friend just rolled her eyes and said people did and felt the same things around *her*. But Leonie didn't believe it.

Dawn—yellow-skinned and pale-eyed—was the ordinary beauty of them, but often complained how she felt like an ugly duckling among black swans.

"Yes, girl," she said. "And we did not want any part of your mother's unhappiness." Dawn straightened the dark blue hat on her short curls.

Verna rolled her eyes. "What this coward is saying is that's the reason she didn't come in to say hello to your parents."

"What's your excuse?" Dawn laughed at her with a flash of slightly crooked teeth. "You didn't say anything to them, either."

"You know Mrs. Harper doesn't like me," Verna muttered.

Leonie nodded. "Very true."

"Anyway, Leonie...." Dawn waved her hand to change the topic as they walked down the drive, arm in arm. "Did they buy the story about college shopping?"

They'd agreed to meet in the city and catch the early reading of one of their favorite poets, a scandalous woman who wrote beautifully about the inspirational properties of erotic love. There was no way the girls could've told their parents that's where they were really going.

"Of course," Leonie said with a shrug. "Otherwise, I wouldn't be here, would I?"

"God!" Verna rolled her eyes, just about her favorite thing to do aside from stealing the boyfriends of her enemies. "You're such a smart ass."

"Better a smart ass than a dumb ass, right?" Leonie bared her teeth at her friend.

They spent the rest of the day in the city proper, met up with another friend who would also be going to Radcliffe come fall semester, and even went shopping for their college outfits before collapsing from combined exhaustion and happiness at an ice cream parlor near the streetcar.

"It's getting late. We should probably get back." Dawn looked unhappily into the last of her vanilla ice cream sundae.

"We don't have to, if we don't want." Verna licked chocolate sauce from her spoon and looked rebellious. "No one here really has a curfew."

True enough. Leonie *shouldn't* stay out past midnight, but if she let her parents know what she was up to, they didn't mind if she came in later. Mostly.

"Sure." Leonie took a bite of her chocolate brownie swimming in a small sea of melted French vanilla ice cream. "What do you girls want to do?"

Verna sucked the spoon in her mouth and looked a little too wicked for Leonie's taste. "Let's go back to that place with the hot fiddle player."

Oh, damn. Leonie clenched her teeth and didn't say anything out loud.

"What's it called?" Dawn drained the last of her ice cream. "Rosie's?"

"It was a little sleazy, though," Leonie said coolly, trying to throw them off track.

Verna gave her a smirking look. "That's why you loved it, remember?"

"Did you ever get that Southern man to sample your cream?" Dawn asked, her smile teasing and merciless.

Her friends burst into giggles while Leonie squirmed, uncomfortable now but trying not to let it show. She scooped the pale ice cream over the chocolate brownie. Golden was all hers. No way would she share him with her friends, even for something as simple as telling them what she and Golden had done together.

She, Verna, and Dawn each had their games. This was, in fact, the thing they reverted to when they were bored—they bet against each other about the men they could lure to their beds.

After making the pact that none of them would go to their wedding nights as virgins, all three girls had discovered the delights of sexual congress and never looked back. They took care of themselves and had precautions in place to protect against pregnancy and disease. They talked openly with each other about sex and anything they didn't understand. They were all, thoroughly, modern women.

Through it all, Leonie had only been with four men, and they were men she'd known most of her life and who didn't want anything beyond the casual coming together of flesh when they needed to scratch an itch.

But Golden wasn't like these others. She actually liked him. Really, really liked him. Beyond wanting the firm touch of his body against hers, she liked the way he laughed with her, liked the syrup-slow drip of his words, and absolutely *loved* how he took care of her, even when she'd given him no reason to.

For him, she would break the honesty pact she had with her friends. "No," she said with a careless shrug. "I didn't really want him, anyway. Remember, it was you guys who dared me to go up to him."

"Yeah, but I saw how you looked when you got back from the alley with him," Verna said. "Like you'd been knocked over by a streetcar." She threw her head back and laughed. "You *like* him."

She tried to deny it again, but her friends ignored her. They teased her mercilessly through the rest of her brownie and ice cream and somehow convinced her that yes, she wanted to go to Rosie's and see Golden play again. With them watching her every second of the night.

What she really wanted was to have him to herself again. Obviously, he didn't like her friends, and, as much as they teased her about him, they wouldn't think too well of her if she decided to go around with him. Hell, she didn't know what she'd think of *herself* if she decided to go around with him. Especially in the way she was used to going around with men. Casually. No strings.

He was a forever type of guy. She saw it in the way he'd looked at her when they were in his bed. He wasn't as casual as the men she'd been with before. And he wouldn't allow himself to be used like that, either.

Leonie was still thinking about this when she, Verna, and Dawn got to Rosie's later that night.

Just like the first and only night they'd been there together, the bar was smoky. Crowded. Loud. Not at all like the places Leonie usually went with the girls. Those places were filled with sedate men, and their smooth manners and almost theatrical ways of approaching the women they wanted, ways which immediately fell away once the men thought they had a chance of getting them into bed.

Golden had been rough from the beginning, crushing Leonie's own theatrical advances. But once he'd gotten her into bed, he'd turned into silk, bringing her to the very heights of pleasure over and over again. Even when his solid maleness pounded between her thighs, he'd been delicate with her. With her feelings, her trust.

As much as those other men promised not to reveal to another soul how Leonie made love, or even that she was "that sort of girl," Golden was the only one she trusted with the unraveling of herself which came from true abandon to pleasure.

She trusted his desire. She trusted him.

"God! I forgot how loud this place is!" Dawn shouted into Leonie's ear once they were at a table near the stage. It wasn't the same table they'd had before, but it was close enough.

A waitress brought them drinks and flirted with every man between their table and the kitchen on her way back to them. A gold tooth flashed from her earthy grin and Leonie's cheeks creased automatically in response.

What in this woman's life made her gorgeously happy? Leonie smiled at the woman's disappearing back and sipped her gin rickey.

On stage, Golden had traded places with the usual piano player and practically danced from his seat. Heaving and sweating bodies already took up the space immediately in front of the stage, and the Ragtime skittered over Leonie's skin like warm fingers. Her foot tapped under the table. The sound from the instruments thrummed in her chest while the woman with the band sang about the virtues of her latest lover.

"This is hot, huh?" Dawn sipped from her drink and swayed in her chair while Verna giggled and pointed at Golden on the stage.

"He sure is!" Verna shouted above the music.

Leonie bit back a sigh. The man was every bit as mouthwatering as she remembered. Maybe more.

Energy poured off him, straight down from the stage. Every movement of his fingers on the piano keys, every ecstatic jerk of his body reverberated through her. Her hands flickered with a strange electricity. She wanted to touch him. Desperately.

She knew the moment Golden saw her. He never lost a beat, if anything the music became even more powerful, pulsing waves of joy moving through the entire club. She felt his eyes on her. Hot. Molten. Lusty.

"If that man could eat you up with his eyes...."

Leonie shook her head, but the smile fighting its way to her lips betrayed her gladness. On stage, Golden played harder. The music got bolder. More joyful.

"Are you sure you didn't put a spell on this one? He looks about ready to propose to you."

"Don't be an idiot." But Leonie blushed. What would that be like, truly? To give herself over to the intense feelings between them and to not worry about her future, or his.

By the time the band took a break, she was breathless with longing. She jumped up from her chair.

"Washroom," she muttered, then quickly stumbled away from the table before her friends could follow.

With only a vague memory of the club's layout guiding her, she found the water closet. Once inside, she splashed water on her face and dried herself with the handkerchief from her purse. The door squeaked open behind her and she turned, an apology for hogging the sink on her lips, but it wasn't another woman wanting to wash her hands.

Golden stood in the dim light of the bathroom, sweat gleaming on his face.

"Leonie...?"

"Yes." It didn't matter what he was asking for. She wanted it, too.

He grabbed her hand and tugged her from the washroom, through a narrow and mostly empty hallway where a few people ignored them as they flew by. Their paired footsteps clattered against the wooden floors, frantic and mad until they finally burst through a heavy door and stumbled into a small, glassed-in room. Rosie's alley and the night lay just outside the dirty and opaque window.

Golden took her waist and pulled her against him. "I didn't think I'd see you today."

"It was my friends' idea."

"So, you didn't want to see me?" His breath huffed against hers, lips close enough to kiss with only a sip of breath between them. But he didn't lean in, and neither did she.

Leonie was getting her breath back, feeling more in control of herself the longer they stood together. That control wouldn't last, though. From the other side of the door, she could hear voices, the in-between breaths of smokers making use of the alley where she'd thrown herself at Golden twice before.

Now, her head was spinning with him. Those rejections were the currency she paid to have him like this now. Panting and hard against her, smiling in delicious invitation. An invitation she couldn't refuse.

So, you didn't want to see me, he'd said.

"What do *you* think?" Slowly, she pulled back from him, reveling in the anticipation pulsing between them.

Golden's hands settled more firmly on her hips. His grin was positively wicked. "What I think is you're the most beautiful woman in the club tonight, and I want to take you home and do more of what we did last night."

"Oh, do you?"

"Yeah...." His voice, molasses-thick, dipped between her legs like a hot tongue. "Last night, did you think about me while lying in your fancy bed?" The slow stroke of his thumbs on her waist unraveled the threads of their conversation, making it hard to follow.

He was so addictive. And she was...she was a mess.

The fog in her brain grew denser with each touch, with each stroke of his fingers on her skin through the dress. Her breath grew rough. Shudders of pre-pleasure tripped through her body.

"Do you have servants feeding you bonbons before you fall asleep to dream about me?"

Huh? She licked her lips and watched his delicious mouth move with words she barely understood. Quivery and sparking hot with desire for him, she was ready to climb all the way out of her skin.

Her head swam, but somehow she suddenly caught up.

"You are so full of yourself." Leonie hated how breathless she sounded. "You're not even half as good as you think."

"Uh-huh."

God, he was driving her crazy. And he knew it. A few inches of space lingered between them, but she could feel every part of his desire for her. Yet he didn't seem as wrecked by it as she was. She needed to get back the control he so effortlessly took from her.

"I don't know what you're talking about, country boy," she murmured and took a step back. "I didn't come out here for this."

"Then what do you want, lioness?" His words dipped into her. Teased. Flirted.

Leonie wet her lips and imagined the taste of his. "All I want is a cigarette."

"Oh, yeah?"

"Yes, country boy. Do you have one for me?" She smiled when his eyes darkened, and victory made her bold. "Can you light me up?"

Still smiling, she dropped to her knees in front of him. He groaned out her name then, the game completely over. Breath stuttering, Golden blinked down at her and she kept those beautiful eyes of his captive while she undid his belt, unbuttoned him. His eyes darkened even further, going black with desire. To have such power over a man like this.... Leonie moaned from the feeling, pressing it tight between her thighs. He squeezed his eyes shut when she reached into his small-clothes and gripped him.

"Holy God...."

"Open your eyes." She kept her touch on his vulnerable flesh firm and steady. "I want to see you."

With Golden's eyes wide open and watching her, Leonie opened her mouth and took him deep inside.

He grunted as if she'd punched the air from his chest.

His taste, salt and sweat and man, was heavy on her tongue. She groaned around his thick weight and felt his reaction trip through her—his lashes fluttering low and that long moan of pleasure. His fingers drifted to her shoulders, then to the back of her neck, resting lightly on her skin as she moved her mouth on him. His essence trickled into her mouth and she swallowed it down.

Panting quietly, Golden caressed the pearls around her throat, then the damp skin of her neck. Her skin buzzed with sensation.

Voices rose and fell in the alley nearby, background noise to the miracle of connection happening between them. Golden's breath puffed hard and urgent with every movement of her mouth. He was slick and hot, perfect between her lips.

She'd done this before, but it had never made her feel as powerful as now, as wanted, as drenched in desire. Between her thighs, she was soaking. Moaning, still meeting his eyes, she tongued the tip of him, circled, and took him deeper.

"Oh, God. Leonie...Jesus. You're—" But his words fell away with the drop of his head against the wall.

She pulled her mouth away with a gentle pop. "Golden, please." Her throat was rough from taking him. "I want to see you." Trembling with her own want, she licked a damp and filthy line up the thick stalk of his sex. "Please. Look at me."

He panted like a long distance runner, thighs trembling beneath her hands. But he opened his eyes and watched her like she asked, and that helpless lust in his molten eyes flooded her with the most perfect conflagration of feeling. His entire body shuddered when her mouth touched him again.

"God, I could love you." He gasped.

No.

A stroke of fear, then unwanted pleasure, tore through her chest. Very easily, she could love him, too.

With a harsh cry, he pulsed in her throat, his essence spurting into her, pouring into her body and filling her up with all the possibilities she'd denied herself up until that very moment.

He groaned her name again, slid down the wall until they were face to face. After looking at her as if she were his own personal miracle, he kissed her long and deep. She smiled against his lips, relishing the taste of his seed on her tongue.

He stroked her cheek, her throat, hand moving down the front of her dress. "I don't know how I'm going to concentrate for the rest of the night."

She squirmed with the touch of his hands on her breast. "We don't have time," she said. "Get back on the stage. I'll take care of myself later."

He drew back, a pleased smile on his face. "Will you? And what if I want to watch and help you just like you helped me?"

She teased him with another kiss, enjoying this simple pleasure, their shared laughter. "Go back to your little garret. Play your beautiful music until we see each other again." His heart beat hard and fast under her palm.

"I don't want to wait until then."

She shrugged. "That has nothing to do with me." Teasing, still.

The voices in the alley on the other side of the wall had mostly drifted away while they'd been busy. Leonie didn't even hear any footsteps. She leaned in to kiss him one last time. "You should probably get back."

His hand skimmed over her belly and, before she knew it, he'd taken her pocket watch to see the time, flipped it back closed, and slid it back into its small pocket. He cursed.

"You're right about that." With a grunt, he quickly stood, helped her to her feet. "Don't leave," he said. "I want to see you after." He squeezed her hips and she shuddered at the possessive clasp of his hands, the burn of him through her clothes.

Swept along on the tide of feeling rushing through her, she could only say one thing. "Yes." Anything he wanted.

"Okay. See you after the show." After another searing look and a quick kiss, he was gone.

But it turned out she couldn't stay. Her friends pulled her from the club, bored when they couldn't find any other so-called "beautiful musicians" to play with. She snapped and complained, but Verna and Dawn eventually got their way.

They ended up at one of their usual places. A genteel club filled with well-mannered gentlemen and a few old school friends they'd kept in touch with. They drank sweet drinks and exchanged plans for the future while she thought about Golden's face when he realized she was gone.

Tomorrow. She would wake up tomorrow and rush downtown to see him before he played at Rosie's again. But even with the decision made, she couldn't stop thinking about him.

What was Golden becoming to her?

This thing between them had to end, but when? And would she be able to let him go when the time came?

By the end of the night, she had no answers to her questions, only the need to see him again. Tomorrow. The honeyed bite of anticipation followed her down into sleep like a haunting lullaby.

11

———

The sound of Leonie's bedroom window sliding open woke her up.

She bolted upright in bed, heart galloping as the sheets tumbled from her shoulders. The sound of her own frightened gasp echoed sharply in the room. Darkness writhed near the window and she bit back a scream, frantically scrabbling under the bed for her croquet mallet, a "weapon" she'd kept nearby since hearing about a break-in a few miles down the road.

"Hush, beautiful girl." The scent of smoke and whiskey blew toward her. A familiar voice. "It's only me."

"Golden?" Her grip on the mallet loosened the same moment she felt a warm weight settle onto the side of her bed. "What are you doing here?" Gradually, her eyes grew used to the darkness enough to see him, shadowy and broad in her room. His gold eyes glowed down at her.

"Were you expecting someone else?" His fingers brushed hers around the mallet and she shivered, making no sound when the so-called weapon fell to the sheets with barely a thud.

He'd climbed through her bedroom window? She gawked at

Golden in the darkness. The window to her room was very high and ringed by a balcony many terrifying feet from the ground.

"I can't believe you're here," she whispered.

"Do you want me to go?" He slid closer and his breath brushed her mouth, gifting her with the scent of whiskey.

He shouldn't be here. Her mother was going to kill her. But her fingers fisted tight in his thin cotton shirt, her other hand already pushing off his jacket.

"You shouldn't be here." But she was so glad to see him. Her pulse beat steadily in her throat, between her legs. Golden was here, in her bed....

"I was barely able to play after you left." His mouth was close to hers still, but not quite close enough. "I couldn't stop thinking about how you smelled, about the way you touched me." His jacket dropped to the bed and she tugged his shirt from the waist of his pants to quickly unbutton it. "You said you would touch herself when you got home and think about me." He gasped when she sank her nails into the hard muscles of his chest. "Did you, beautiful girl?"

God...she wanted to tell him a filthy lie about making herself orgasm all alone in her bed while thinking of him. But the words wouldn't come.

Leonie tilted her head back to look at the shadowing online of him. "What do you think?" She touched his soft skin over hard muscles. "Were you thinking about me touching myself while you were on the streetcar?"

"Sweetheart, if I did, I would've made a mess all in my trousers." He moved from her bed, graceful and efficient, quickly taking off the rest of his clothes and then helping with hers until they were both naked. "I came to get you off, baby. I've already had mine."

Mercy, he knew just the right words to say.

Leonie groaned out her eagerness and raked her fingernails over his naked chest, scraping his nipples along the way. Golden's breath stuttered on her name.

"You talk so sweet, Golden. Almost as sweet as you taste. Thanks for giving me some of your sugar earlier today at Rosie's."

His shocked and pleased moan curved a smile on her lips. She kissed the corner of his mouth, bit his chin, and scraped her teeth over the evening stubble there. Her belly twisted in sympathetic pleasure when he moaned deep and low. This man was so gorgeous. So amazing.

The things she felt with him made her think this was what flying felt like, soaring among the clouds with nothing but heaven above and a magical lightness to her very being.

What would it be like to feel like this all the time? To simply roll over or turn her head or look across the room and receive his smile, the incredible jubilation he caused in her very spirit?

She was being greedy, Leonie knew. None of this could last. But while she had it, she wanted it. God, she wanted it. "Give me some more."

He settled between her thighs and rubbed himself between her wet folds until she was practically begging him to come inside. "I have everything you need right here, baby."

Then he gave it to her. Slowly, firmly, he fed her the hard silk of his sex, grunting from the urgent rapture but did not rush. Leonie took him in, greedy in her eagerness. As he began to move, she moaned his name and clasped her legs around him. She clung, and gasped, and shivered as he rocked into her, fiercely ringing that magical bell inside her to make her cry out in gladness.

"Leonie." He groaned her name. "Leonie...."

Gasp after gasp left her throat, each louder than the last. Never in her life had Leonie been so grateful to have a room at the farthest end of the hallway.

Between her thighs, Golden was relentless and beautiful. Only after he'd shaken her apart three times did he follow her over into bliss. His entire body shuddered in the grip of a merciless and pulsing wave, and Leonie held onto him tighter as his pleasure triggered another orgasm. Her trembling hands clutched his back and slid in the river of sweat over his writhing muscles. She bit down into his shoulder and wailed her completion into his skin, all of her shaking helplessly beneath the most perfect lover she'd ever had.

"I'm never going to let you go," she gasped when she could speak again. "Never."

12

"Do you mean what you said before?"

The open window allowed in a breeze that stroked its cool fingers over Leonie's sweat-dampened back. Sprawled as she was on the furnace of Golden's body, she didn't want to move. He'd knocked every sense out of her head with his beautiful penis.

"Hmm?" She hummed the question, even though she knew very well what he was talking about. Her stupid sex confession.

"Don't play with me, Leonie girl." His fingers caressed her hip, drifted over her bottom and up to her back in a rhythm hovering perfectly between soothing and arousing. "Is for keeps what you're after?"

She bit her lip and closed her eyes. This thing she had with Golden was too beautiful to last, and too delicate to survive in the world she lived. It was easy enough to ignore while they rolled around in the sheets together, but the truth of it remained stronger than ever.

Very carefully, she pulled back and rolled away to drop down beside him on her stomach.

"I want you."

Leonie didn't think she'd said it out loud until he responded. "I want you, too, Leonie girl."

This wasn't fair. Suddenly, the wind on her skin felt cold, icy instead of soothing. Why was she doing this to herself? To Golden?

"This thing between us can't work, though." She tried for honesty and hoped the pain from it wouldn't be too much. "We—we don't have a future in common." Hurt twisted in her chest, too tight and sharp for her to ignore. Although she hadn't realized it before, she wanted this thing. But it couldn't work.

"It can work if we want it to." Golden tugged her back onto of him, widening his thighs for her to slip between them. They fell naturally together, hip to hip, heart to heart. "I want you, you want me. There's nothing else to think about." Soothing fingers trailed down the back of her neck and over her shoulders. "All that matters is us. My mama always said as long as you decide to journey together, getting to your destination is easy."

That was exactly the problem. She knew where she was heading, and it wasn't to a place Golden could follow.

Cambridge, Massachusetts. Its moneyed Ivy League university, the snobs she'd grown up with—that was where she belonged. And that place would be as alien to Golden as the country lanes of his southern birthplace would be for her. She didn't want to be there, herself. She could only imagine how he'd react to it.

With a shuddering sigh, she clung to him and pressed her lips into his chest. His heart beat fiercely under her mouth. He tasted of the salt of their pleasure. A soothing hum left his lips and rippled like love along her skin to the same delicious rhythm of his hand gliding down her neck and back. Shivering from that stolen pleasure, Leonie buried her face in his warm skin and imagined the scent of peaches mingling with the rancid reluctance rising from her own skin.

And, for a few moments, she pretended it was enough.

Sometime before dawn, he climbed out of her room, leaving her a note and the vague memory of a kiss. Hours later, she woke sore and sated. And guilty.

· · ·

You're too beautiful to worry, he'd written on the cream stationary he'd found her desk. *I'm working on a plan. Getting there together will be easy, you'll see. – G*

Three mornings later, she still hadn't recovered from Golden's nighttime visit when the maid came to the family room and announced her friends' appearance in the front parlor.

"Thank you, Carlotta." She put her book aside and tuned in to what else was going on in the room.

Sitting side by side on the long sofa, her parents were still talking about the Negro jockey, Jimmy Winkfield, who'd won the Kentucky Derby the night before. It was another Negro success that shook the hornet's nest of whites' assumed superiority. Some white southerners were already complaining that Negroes were taking over an honorable white sport. Her father rolled his eyes.

"We do one thing they consider good, and they think we're trying to take over their whole world," he said with a bitter laugh. "The way they act, if they don't get credit for everything good, they want to burn the Earth to ashes."

"I wish that was even mildly funny, Martin," Leonie's mother said. "Who knows what these people will do now?"

Before they could get into another of their "healthy debates," Leonie called out her goodbyes and left to meet her friends at the door.

Church was long over and she was heading out with Dawn, Verna, and some boys they knew from school. The guys were supposed to be here any moment now in their new automobile.

"I still think we should see a picture," Dawn said, straightening her hat in front of the parlor mirror. She already looked pretty in a pale green blouse with the waterfall of delicate lace down her throat and chest. She yelped when Verna dragged her away from the mirror and toward the door.

"We went to the picture you wanted last time," Verna said with a toss of her long hair. "It's Leonie's turn to pick."

"She doesn't care," Dawn said. "Her head is still in the clouds, for a reason we can only imagine." Her sly smile had a touch of jealousy to it.

Leonie rolled her eyes. This had nothing to do with the things she felt for Golden.

She fluffed the three-quarter length sleeves of her dress, a yellow-gold color that was now her favorite, and headed for the front door behind her friends. "*Paganini in Love* is showing today." It was a play by one of Radcliffe's more famous graduates. "How about we go there instead of the movies?"

Both her friends groaned.

"Come on, Leonie...." Dawn made a sound like a dog being put down and gave Leonie a sour look over her shoulder. "Just because we're going to Radcliffe in the fall doesn't mean you have to be boring right now. We'll be giving up our lives to the college soon enough as it is."

"Oh my God, we're not giving anything up," Leonie said, trying to mean every word. "You two make it sound as if our parents are forcing us to go to one of the best—if not *the* best—women's colleges in the country. Radcliffe will be lucky to have us, but we're also very lucky to have Radcliffe. It'll open up the world to us. Remember Ginnie Scott?"

They trooped into the vestibule, Verna still gripping Dawn's arm, Leonie just behind them.

"God! Between you and my parents...," Verna growled. "If I hear about Alberta Virginia Scott one more damn time—"

"There's no point in waiting," Leonie interrupted her jealous rant. She was dreading going up to Cambridge enough as it was. She just needed to do it, like jumping into a frigid pool. Radcliffe was inevitable. Despite the sadness of the decision curling around her like noxious smoke, there was no way to avoid it. No matter how Golden made her feel. "We're going to be at the college in a couple of months, we might as well get ourselves ready."

"There is no one here who cares to see you, *sir*."

At the unusually sharp sound of the maid's voice, Leonie flicked a narrowed gaze toward the front door. Who was Carlotta talking to so rudely? Frowning, she hurried the last few steps to the door.

Golden stood in the open doorway, staring at Leonie. "You're leaving Washington?"

She stumbled to an abrupt stop.

He looked...amazing.

He was handsome, even taller than usual in a suit she'd never seen him in before. His hair was freshly cut and brushed in waves clinging to his beautiful head like water at low tide. His tie was the same shade as his eyes. Eyes now a darker shade than Leonie had seen in a long time. They snapped with anger. Betrayal.

He held a bouquet of white peonies in one hand.

"Yes, she's going away to college in Massachusetts," Dawn said before Leonie could unstick her tongue from the roof of her mouth to answer. She was obviously still mad about not getting her way.

Golden ignored her, his molten eyes focused completely on Leonie. "You didn't tell me you were leaving."

Leonie swallowed. She still couldn't say anything. Her face grew colder by the moment. Her tongue was like lead.

Snap out of it! Say something! But her mouth wouldn't move.

"Does this piece of tail think you're going to give up Radcliffe just to lie around in his bed and take his prick all day?" Dawn's vicious words yanked her out of her paralysis, but not in time to stop Verna from joining in.

"You're just a summer stopover, country boy," Verna chimed in, and that somehow seemed worse than what Dawn said.

Leonie turned to her friends. "Stop it!"

She should say something to Golden. He was the one who deserved her attention and apology, but she didn't know what to say. How could she explain what she was doing to him? To herself?

"Are they telling the truth?" He snapped the question, brittle and sharp. "Tell it to me straight, Leonie."

Her shoulders sagged under the weight of what she needed to say, but she was her mother's daughter enough to say it. "Yes." She turned to him, her head high and regret in her eyes. "I'm leaving for school soon."

"Okay. I suppose that's it, then." He turned to go, then stopped. His wide shoulders straightened before he turned back to her. "These are for you." He held out his hands with the flowers and, moving like a puppet under another's control, she took them. Their scent was sweet and pungent, funeral blossoms atop the corpse of what had once been beautiful between them.

A cry of pain rose up in her throat, but she bit her tongue, stifling it. The taste of blood filled her mouth. When Golden turned his back to her and began striding away down the drive, the sweet scent of the peonies choked her and made her cough. Or was it a sob?

She wanted to call out to him, beg him not to leave. Each step he took away from her sharpened the pain, slashed like a knife in a place she couldn't touch.

Shit, shit, shit.

"I'll be right back." She tossed the words at her friends, tossed the flowers to the maid, and ran after him. Her heels clicked desperately on the driveway. "Golden!"

But when he stopped, the words she'd half-thought up dried up on her tongue.

"I'm sorry," she choked out.

"You don't look sorry to me. All I see on your face is relief, like what I felt for you is trash you're glad to get rid of."

Felt. He was done with her. It shouldn't have hurt so much, but it did. "I have to go away. I don't have a choice."

"A girl like you? I don't believe it. As much as you talked about my choice to play at Rosie's instead of the fancy places you and your folks like to show off in? Nope. Unless you're thinking people like me are the only ones who don't live up to their so-called potential." He threw her words back in her face from a few days before. He turned away, cursing beneath his breath, but she caught the flare of pain in his bright eyes and, God, it burned. "I just wish you'd told me before I fell for you."

But it wasn't that simple. "I didn't know!"

"You didn't know what, exactly? That I'd fall for you after you'd practically shoved the damn ladder from under my feet? Fuck, Leonie...." He growled, low and rough. "Fuck!"

Just then, she heard the putter of a motor car and, moments later, an automobile pulled into the driveway. Verna's latest boyfriend, Weston, was driving while his two friends sat beside him. She and Golden automatically stepped aside and onto the grass to let it pass. The wind ruffled Weston's loose curls, and he gave her a jaunty wave and pulled up closer to the house where Verna and Dawn waited.

"You should get going," Golden spat. "My replacement is waiting."

This time, when he walked away, she didn't try to stop him.

Leonie had a reputation to uphold, even among her close friends, so she went into town. She watched the movie and ate popcorn while trying to act like nothing was wrong. Like she was the same person—unhurt, unchanged—who'd walked out of the house and stumbled into Golden with his flowers in his hand and his heart in his eyes.

But she wasn't that girl.

At home, she made her excuses for dinner and ran up to her room. After taking a quick bath, she huddled in the sheets still thick with the sweat of the two of them, of her and Golden. It was torture.

She pushed her back to the headboard, the same place he'd pressed her wrists together and made forceful, perfect love to her. If she closed her eyes, she could feel it all again. Every caress. Every thrust. Every cry of his name past her parted lips.

The room's silence rang with the memory of her words to him.

I'm never going to let you go, she'd said.

But she'd lied. Before morning, she'd already released him and, now, he was as far away as the moon. Foolish, unwise words. Her heart saying what it wanted.

It was too much. The tentacles of the sheets twisted around her legs, but she fought them and climbed frantically from the bed. She tumbled to the floor with a gasp, hands flat against the cool hardwoods.

There, that was better.

No pillow. No sheets. Just her misery. And her stupidity.

Oh, God. Golden. The future she was just beginning to think could be hers.

A long while later, a knock on her bedroom door jolted her from her stupor.

"Leonie!" Anna's fierce whisper reached her through the door. "Open up! I know you're in there."

But she didn't answer. After calling her name too many more times for Leonie to count, Anna eventually went away.

Then another knock came.

"Leonie Harper." Her father's voice, low but authoritative, came through the door. "May I speak with you for a moment?"

Papa? What did he want?

She sat up, wiping away the tears she hadn't realized were falling until she tasted salt. Reaching out with trembling hands, she pressed her fingers against the floor and levered herself slowly to her feet. She staggered and cried out when she nearly fell. The long hours on the floor hadn't done her any favors. After a quick glance to make sure nothing damning lay on her bed, she hobbled to the door and carefully opened it.

"Of course, Papa." She cleared her throat and led him to her small, attached sitting room. "What's on your mind?"

"You are, my dear." He took the seat at her writing desk, his big body dwarfing the delicate Louis XV-style chair. "Your sister says you aren't answering the door. You've been up here for quite a while. I'm worried."

Leonie curled up in the overstuffed chaise under the window and wrapped her arms around her upraised legs. Her skin felt raw and vulnerable. And she felt too tender to lie.

"It's nothing I won't get over, Papa." She balanced her chin on her knees and nibbled on her bottom lip so he wouldn't see its wobble.

"Do you want to tell me what's wrong?"

She shook her head. "Not really."

A faint smile touched her father's face, but it was a sad one. "Let me put it another way. Please tell me what's going on with you. Otherwise, your mother will barge up here and try to harangue it out of you."

Misery squeezed her eyes shut. Nausea twisted in her stomach at the very thought of her mother talking *at* her.

"It's..." *A man. It's my life. It's everything.*

"I don't want to go to Cambridge in the fall," she said. And it felt like such a relief to finally say the words.

"What?" To call the look on her father's face 'shock' would've been an understatement. "You've been planning on Radcliffe since... for years."

"No, *Mama* has been planning this for me."

A frown settled between his brows, and questions, one after the other, flew across his expressive face. Finally, he linked his fingers over a crossed knee. "So, you don't want to go in the fall, or you don't want to go ever?"

"I don't want the college at all, I want...I want something else." Embarrassment burned her cheeks. It seemed stupid, she knew, this reluctance to do something another girl in her position would kill for. Hell, she should have waited until she had some sort of alternative before confessing this. Having no other plan was fine for someone like Anna. But for her?

"If you don't want to attend Radcliffe, what do you want, daughter?"

"I don't know, Papa. I just want the freedom to find it for myself."

Her father nodded thoughtfully. "Your mother has a strong will." He said nothing else for a few long moments, only looked at her with a considering light in his eyes, thumb tapping against his pocket watch, a habit she realized, just then, that she'd gotten from him.

Finally, he spoke again. "Leonie, I didn't fight for the life we have now just for my children to suffer beneath the weight of another's control. You going to Radcliffe would do our family proud. You'd be one of the first Negro women to matriculate and graduate. But I won't have you do this if it will kill your spirit."

What? This whole time, was that all she'd had to say? Leonie swallowed thickly. It wasn't as if she didn't know her father was a better listener than her mother—much more enlightened, a man who saw more to the world than simple status—but this confirmed it.

"But although I understand what you want, it won't be enough for your mother."

"I know." It wasn't a conversation she looked forward to. But it couldn't be any more painful than watching Golden walk away from her. "But I have to make her understand."

"Yes, you do."

13

"What do you mean, you don't want to go to Radcliffe?" Her mother's voice lashed through the closed study.

Leonie flinched but stiffened her spine. After her father left, she'd gone down to see her mother, armed with the knowledge of her father's support. But he'd disappeared by the time she got downstairs, abandoning her to face her mother alone.

"Just what I said."

Leonie stood in front of her mother's desk with her hands clasped in front of her. Her mother sat behind the desk, confronting Leonie's gaze with a steady and direct one of her own. The lamps in the room illuminated her mother's unyielding beauty. Her thick hair was pulled back from her face in a curly corona, her dress impeccable and crisp, even at ten o' clock at night.

Under her dress, Leonie's knees quaked.

They stared at each other and, looking at her mother, Leonie realized what Golden had meant when he said she sometimes had glaciers in her eyes. Her mother leveled the coldness of the entire polar ice cap at her. Only a stiff spine and a lifetime of dealing with her mother's frightening will kept her from cowering and backing away. That, and the sips of gin she'd taken just before coming downstairs.

"Your sister told me you met a man."

Leonie's spine abruptly turned to jelly. She was going to kill Anna. "What?"

Her mother stood and moved from behind the desk, her skirts swishing around her long legs in a whisper of sound as terrifying as a snake's rattle. She came to a stop only a few feet from Leonie.

"Anna told me a few days ago you were out until early morning." Annoyance disturbed the deceptively placid beauty of her face. "I know you're a responsible girl, so I didn't say anything to you. I trust you not to let a man ruin your chances of a good future." Her mother clasped her hands at her waist and looked down at Leonie from her slight advantage in height. "Have I misplaced my trust in you, daughter?"

Leonie's cold hands trembled. Words flashed through her mind, thoughts of what she could say to deny anything her sister said. But as much of a betrayer Anna was, she wasn't a liar, and their mother already knew this.

"This has nothing to do with him," Leonie said.

A sneer pulled at her mother's mouth. "Really? So you weren't perfectly content to go to Radcliffe—the best women's college in this country—until you met this man you snuck into your bed and fornicated with while the rest of us were asleep?"

Oh my God!

"I...." Leonie clenched her teeth to stop any senseless babbling. She took a breath and, once she felt able to make complete sentences again, plowed on. "I never wanted to go. I told you." The rising whine she heard in her own voice made her sound like a wounded child, but Leonie couldn't stop now. "Radcliffe is what you want for me. Just like you wanted Wallace to attend Harvard."

Her mother hissed, a boiling kettle of a sound that scuttled alarm down Leonie's back. "How dare you mention your brother to me?" The question nearly pushed her down into the chair her mother had insisted on—but she refused to take—at the beginning of the interrogation. Nearly, but not quite.

She mirrored her mother's aggressive pose, hands on her hips, teeth bared in anger. "How dare you push the life you had in mind for him onto me?"

In the Harper household, nobody ever talked about Wallace. The oldest and the only boy, he was the one their parents once had the highest hopes for. But he'd died on a boating trip while fooling around with some of his prep school friends, taking Leonie's independence and her mother's already infrequent smiles with him.

"I can't be him, Mama. I just can't!"

"I never asked you to be."

"That's true, you never *asked* me. You just told me."

With her brother's death and her mother's constant pressure for Leonie to step into the void he created, Leonie had never thought of anything else she wanted except to climb from beneath the incredible weight of becoming the replacement Golden Child.

Golden. Her thoughts stuttered.

"Is that what you've felt all these years?"

It took her a few seconds to refocus on the conversation. "Yes...yes it is. You never said or did anything to prove me wrong."

"Well, you *are* wrong." Her mother abruptly stepped away, kicking aside the skirts of her dress like a flamenco dancer, the movement sharp and angry.

Hands clenched into fists at her side, Leonie followed her. "You can't tell me what I feel, Mama. It doesn't work that way."

"Listen to me, young woman—"

"Helen, why are you shouting at our daughter?" Her father appeared in the doorway, making Leonie jump. Behind him, Anna's frightened eyes peered at them.

"I'm not shouting at her. She's simply talking nonsense."

"Really? I'm reasonably sure I heard both your raised voices from my study."

So he hadn't left her completely alone. Leonie sagged with relief.

"Your father isn't going to save you, Leonie," her mother snapped.

"Save?" Her father straightened and stepped into the room. "That makes it sound like you intend for some harm to come to her. What's going on here?"

Helen turned her sharp gaze to the door. "I think you know exactly what's going on here, Martin. Did you put her up to this?"

"Up to what, exactly?" His voice remained level, but his eyes flashed dangerously.

His wife ignored the warning and turned to Leonie in a swirl of blue skirts. "She wants to throw Radcliffe away because of some man." She practically spat the last word, contempt in every rigid line of her body.

"Mama, it's not—"

"Lower your voice, Leonie." Her father's calm tone instantly made her feel like an ass.

"Sorry, Papa." She clenched her hands behind her back and dug her nails into her own skin hard enough to hurt. "I didn't come in here to start any trouble, I promise. I just...I just want to have my own life again."

"You *have* a life! You have more advantages than most people in this entire city. Definitely more than the man you brought into this house."

"You had a man here?" Leonie's father leveled his eyes on her and she dipped her head, biting her lip hard.

"She didn't tell you any of that, did she? Now you know she's only acting like a cheap—"

"Be very careful what you say, Helen!" her father warned. "This is our child you're talking about. *My* child."

Her mother sucked in her breath sharply. "She doesn't want to go the best women's college in the United States. That doesn't make any sense to me. She'll give up this opportunity for a man who probably—"

"I'm giving it up for me," Leonie said quietly. "No one else."

"To do what, sit on some front porch down South and push out his babies? No!" Pacing from one side of the room to the other, her mother growled her denial. "Not my child."

"She is *our* child, Helen, no matter what. Don't treat her like your parents treated you."

Her mother drew in a harsh breath and stopped. The skirts of her dress swished around her legs, still moving though she had turned to a statue in the middle of the lamp-lit room.

It was the family's open secret. At eighteen, her mother walked away from her parents to be with the man who was now her husband. For them, his skin was too dark to mix with the pale sepia shades of their family. It hadn't mattered to them that Martin Harper, already on the fast track to becoming one of the most influential lawyers in the North, came from an old and very wealthy family. They wanted Helen to lighten the family skin tone, not darken it. Furious that they were trying to tell her how to live her life and how to love, Helen left her family to marry the man she couldn't live without.

Her family had eventually changed its tune, but Helen didn't allow them around her own children. Their backward notions about skin color and shade privilege were noxious diseases she hadn't wanted Anna, Leonie, and Wallace to catch.

In the thunderous silence, Leonie's father spoke again.

"Allow her to make her own choices, Helen. We want for our children the same thing we've always wanted for ourselves. Don't take away your love for her just because she doesn't do what you say."

"But that's not...that's not what I'm doing. Is it?" She looked broken for a moment, nothing like the fierce Amazon ready to tear Leonie from limb to limb because she wanted to choose her own life.

"It is, love."

With a cry, her mother fell into her husband's arms. Leonie's mouth dropped open in shock. She didn't know how long she stood there, listening to her mother's harsh sobs. It was too much. Her mother's pain and vulnerability tore at her. With sickness twisting in her belly, she left them and escaped to her room.

She was sitting on her bed, staring into space, when a timid knock sounded on her door.

Her eyes were stone dry. Not knowing who to expect—her

mother and an apology? Her father and his repeated acceptance?—she called out to whoever it was to come in.

She was wrong on both counts.

"What do you want, Anna?"

"I'm sorry!" Her sister slipped into the room and shut the door. "I'm sorry I told. I didn't mean to."

Leonie rolled her eyes. "You did exactly what you meant to, and you know it."

"But I didn't mean for you and Mama to argue so badly, or for her to cry."

"As usual, you don't think about the consequences of your actions until it's too damn late."

"Please don't be mad. Please." Tears glittered in her sister's eyes. She twisted her fingers together as she shifted from foot to foot, miserable.

Leonie sagged—all anger gone. This was nobody's fault but hers. So what if Anna told their parents about Golden? Leonie was the one who'd been with him and kept it a secret.

"It's okay, Anna. I shouldn't have asked you to lie for me about this."

Her sister sank to the floor at Leonie's feet, tears now flowing down her cheeks. "Are you sure? Because I can...." Anna looked frantically around the room. "I can shine your shoes, or something."

Leonie rubbed her temples and squeezed her eyes shut. "You don't have to do anything. This is my mess." She'd screwed things up with everyone. Her mother. Golden.

A swift and sharp pain flared in her chest. It was nothing she didn't deserve. She'd hurt him so badly with her arrogance and stupidity.

Oh, God. The look on his face when he'd walked away from her the last time. She'd done that to him. But how else could their affair have ended?

From that first night in the alley outside Rosie's, lust had fizzled and popped between them. Falling into bed with him once should have been a scratch for a temporary itch, but it only made her want more. One kiss took her breath away, and only with another taste of his hungry lips could she breathe again.

During and after their sex, he'd said the most amazing things to her. Sweet and cherishing words she hadn't known she craved until he poured them over her like the finest wine. He was everything in a man she'd been missing.

He'd challenged her to admit she wanted him for more than sex.

He'd challenged her to admit she wanted more from her life.

He'd challenged her in every way. And she wanted to keep him in her life.

"I'm going to tell him."

"What?" Anna's confused question jerked Leonie from her thoughts. "What did you just say?"

"Oh, I...I'm going to fix something I broke. At least, I'll try." If it wasn't too late.

"Good." Her sister wiped away the last of her lingering tears, the worry gone from her eyes like clouds from a suddenly sunny sky. "Can I help?"

"Not really, I—" A knock at the door cut her off. Anna met her eyes and shrugged. "Come in," Leonie called out.

The door creaked open and her mother stepped through it. Aside from the slight redness in her eyes, she looked like the same strong and indomitable woman Leonie had known all her life. She released a quiet breath of relief. Her mother was not broken. But where did this leave her?

Leonie's fingers twisted together in her lap.

"Hello, girls." Her mother's voice was only a little rougher than usual, the only other sign of her previous tears. "Leonie, I would like to talk with you alone for a few minutes."

"Of course, Mama."

Anna quickly got to her feet, and, after squeezing Leonie's hand, she left the room, closing the door quietly behind her.

The bed seemed too intimate for their conversation, so Leonie invited her mother into the sitting room. There, she took a seat at her writing desk while her mother sank into the comfortable chair by the window. It was the exact reverse of the position she'd taken with her father only a few hours before.

Not knowing what to expect, Leonie didn't want to get too comfortable. She clasped her hands in her lap and squeezed her fingers together. The butterflies in her stomach fluttered wildly, rushing around inside her like they were caught in a storm. "What's on your mind, Mama?"

"I want to apologize for how unfair I've been to you," her mother said, immediately getting to the point. "I had no idea you feel this way about Radcliffe, but I should have listened to you instead of treating you the way my parents treated me." She took a breath. "From what your father told me, you're...completely rudderless, but you have the right to steer your own boat as you see fit. I can't have you hate—" She sighed. "I can't have you feel the same way about me as I do my own parents."

Leonie released the breath she'd been holding forever. Something inside her that had been clenched so tightly for years slowly relaxed. Her mother's apology wasn't ideal. She wasn't "rudderless," as her mother put it, she just didn't want someone else to guide her life. Once the reins were back in her hands, maybe then she'd have a clear idea of what she wanted to do.

"Thank you, Mama. It means a lot to me to hear you say this."

Her mother let out an audible breath, an echo of Leonie's sigh. "I'm sorry we couldn't have had this conversation sooner. The last thing I want is for any of my children to be unhappy."

Leonie nodded and bit her lip. "So, what now?" This was important. She pressed back into the chair to stop herself from leaning forward. "Where do we go from here?"

She could practically see her mother mentally shift back to familiar ground. Helen Harper sat up straight in the chair and pinned Leonie with her usual, direct stare. "We should answer some basic questions first. Do you even want to go to college?"

"I...I don't. At least, not yet. First, I want to breathe knowing my next breath is not restricted by what you expect."

"Okay." Her mother winced but did not look away. "I'll do whatever you need to make that happen. All I want is for our family to stay a family. I love you and Anna, and Martin. That won't change, no matter the path you choose to follow." Her mother stood and approached Leonie, and Leonie met her halfway. "Okay?"

For the first time in a long while, Leonie felt as if she could truly breathe. "More than okay."

Then she slipped her arms around her mother's waist and held on.

14

It took two days for Leonie to untangle herself from the Radcliffe mess to her mother's satisfaction. That meant canceling her enrollment at the college, talking it through with her parents, and coming to terms with the decision herself. With all that, she wasn't able to leave and find Golden until Wednesday afternoon.

And she was just about too nervous to think straight.

With anxiety fluttering high in her throat, she got off the streetcar in his neighborhood and made her way through half-remembered streets toward his front door. That last time she saw him, she'd been an idiot. Hopefully, he would allow her to explain, or to beg his forgiveness. Though she was a wreck inside, she forced herself to at least look calm: her watch was neatly tucked into the pocket of her dress, her hat at a smart angle, her speech ready.

At his door, she took a deep breath, then knocked.

When nothing happened, she knocked again. Then again.

A glance at her watch confirmed the time. He wasn't due to be at Rosie's until much later, and he should've already finished working at the restaurant. She'd taken a quick peek inside on the way up just to be sure.

Maybe she hadn't been as clever as she thought in timing her visit.

Leonie took the letter she'd written him out of her purse, getting ready to slide it under his door.

She nearly jumped out of her skin when a door across the narrow hallway opened.

"What's this ruckus out here?" a gravelly voice barked. An old woman peeked out from her apartment, narrowed eyes focused on Leonie.

"I'm looking for Golden," Leonie said. At the woman's blank look, she clarified, "The man who lives in this apartment. Is he at work?"

"No idea where he is, girlie. He don't live there no more. He moved out yesterday with a whole lot of fuss and commotion."

Leonie's stomach dropped. "You must be mistaken," she choked out.

The woman snorted. "Right. Good luck finding him, then." She slammed her door in Leonie's face.

"Wait!" Acting on her sudden desperation, Leonie rushed to the woman's door and rapped her gloved knuckles against the hard wood.

"I'm sorry," she said when the woman didn't immediately come to the door. "I didn't mean to be rude, I just…. You just surprised me, that's all." She knocked again, furiously swallowing past the solid ball of dread lodged in her throat. "Can you tell me where he went?" She knocked again, a milder version of her earlier desperate taps. "Please."

The door abruptly opened, almost tumbling Leonie inside the little apartment. Standing in the doorway with a glass of what smelled like gin in her hand, the woman looked both put-upon and smug. "Not so high and might now, are you?"

"I'm sorry, can you just tell me what happened?"

Narrowed eyes filled with judgment looked Leonie up and down. "You're the girl he had over the other day, aren't you? I could hardly sleep because of the way you two were carrying on."

For the love of…

"Yes, I am." She made her voice low and soothing, like her father sometimes did to get her mother to act right. "Can you tell me anything about him leaving?"

"I'll just tell you this. He packed up like the hounds of hell were after him." The woman gave Leonie another smug look and slurped from her glass of gin. Ice tinkled merrily in the glass. "Looked like he was trying to escape something...or some*body*. Put that in your fancy tea and drink it, missy." The woman giggled, an oddly girlish sound, and slammed the door again.

The woman was wrong. She had to be.

Leonie rushed across the hallway, back to Golden's door. In desperation, she grabbed the doorknob. It clicked, turned, and opened.

The apartment was empty, still furnished with the bed and bureau, but the mattress had been stripped. The photo of Golden's mother. His guitar. Everything that had made it Golden's home. All gone.

Waves of hot and cold rolled through Leonie. She stared at the half-crumpled letter in her hand. Her explanation. Her apology. Her begging his forgiveness. There was no one to give it to.

He was really gone.

15

———

*T*hree months later

France wasn't what Golden expected.

Turquoise water. White people everywhere. A warm welcome and the invitation to stay, which was what shocked him most.

These were the things Nelson Biggers had promised him, but Golden's own expectations had all been wrapped up in a certain woman.

Wrapped up. Tied up. Messed up.

Now that she wasn't with him, all he had in this new country was music.

Leonie Harper was an ocean away and would never be with him now. But that didn't stop her from crawling into his dreams every night. He saw her not like she was on the last day at her house—cold and unreachable—but as she was before, fierce and sensual, demanding his touch, his kisses. His love. Everything he'd given to her like a fool.

"All right, now!" The booming voice on the stage next to Golden urged on the entire band and jerked him from his self-pity.

He threw himself into the frenzy of his piano. The keys flew under his fingers and kept up with the rest of the band even when his mind wandered too damn far away.

There were five of them, from three different countries—Haiti, the U.S., and, of course, France. They took over the stage of the ritzy Marseilles nightclub, mixing up Ragtime, African drums, and whatever else they could come up with to create an orgy of sound. The French crowd was wild for it.

The younger ones danced where they could find the space, rocking and bumping hips. The ones who were older and more settled into their skin sat back at their tables, drank wine and smoked their cigarettes, clapped, laughed, and just kept paying to come to the waterfront club night after night.

It felt good to be wanted.

Golden's pockets were practically overflowing with cash, and his little sea-side apartment stayed warm and comfortable. After years of struggle, he now had more than enough.

Music rat-a-tat-tatted in his brain, and his body rolled with the sounds and vibrations from the piano he pounded his rage and sadness into. He plunged deep into the music, played it hard and played it long, until the sweat dripped from every inch of his body. At the end of it, though, he was still waiting for the sore spot in his heart to heal.

"Damn, that was good!" Etienne, their Haitian bandleader, pounded a farewell beat on the djembe between his knees, gave the drum a find caress, and stood.

Golden looked up. The lights burned brightly in the club and the sweating, joyful crowd heaved its way as one toward the door. Conversation rolled through the emptying space. The music was over, and Golden had sleepwalked through it all.

Damn. He needed to get it together.

"You feeling all right, Golden?" Jacques, the regular piano player who'd asked for a break to play the guitar tonight, squeezed his shoulder. They were a touchy-feely bunch. "You seem distracted, more so than usual."

Golden dismissed the man's concern with a smile. "Never better." He could've been more convincing, but he didn't care much right now.

He grabbed his guitar from the back of the stage and slipped it into its case. As he checked the case's latch, something shifted in the thinning crowd and drew his attention. His chest tightened, and it suddenly felt like he'd fallen from the height of a thousand stairs.

No. It couldn't be.

Heart pounding, he jumped from the stage with his guitar slung across his back.

"Hey, *mon ami!* Pascale's?" Etienne called out to him, mentioning the breakfast place they often tumbled into after their sets.

Just about every morning, they went there, laughing over coffee, cigarettes, and eggs, none of them sleepy and all of them wanting to hang out just a little longer before heading home to the family or the girl. Or the lonely apartment at the end of a now-familiar street.

"Naw, man." Golden waved off his friend. "Tomorrow."

"It's already tomorrow." But the big man only returned the wave and turned to leave with the others.

Golden was already walking away, cutting through the emptying club and toward the door. He headed for the phantom who had somehow followed him across the ocean.

Leonie.

Pale dress, glowing skin, red lips. Her cool and dark eyes like the universe where he never belonged.

If he talked to her in the middle of this place, he was going to do something stupid, something embarrassing. It couldn't be here. His heart thudding fast and loud as a djembe, he brushed past her without talking—and, *Christ*, the brief touch of her bare arm against his was electric. He practically ran out the door.

She followed him, a slender and silent shadow.

The night sparkled with laughter, the hiss and whisper of the language he was trying to learn. A man bumped Leonie's shoulder and he begged her pardon, and she engaged him with a smile and a burst of French that, somehow, didn't surprise Golden. They walked farther away from the noise, deeper into the darkness where night met the early morning.

"You sounded good up there," she finally said when they'd been walking for a while. The crowd had long thinned and now only the low streetlamps surrounded them.

A pair of dogs loped ahead on the cobblestoned street. Feminine laughter burst out from a nearby open doorway. Golden's heart tripped over itself.

"What are you doing here, Leonie?" He was too tired to play games.

She pressed her lips into a painful-looking red line. Her chin wobbled and her eyes glinted with the threat of tears.

He stopped and stared as she continued past him.

No, this wasn't the Leonie he was used to. For the woman he'd touched and missed more than he thought possible, composure was everything. This...this wasn't her. His stomach twisted into knots and he wanted nothing more than to pull her into his arms. Instead, Golden shoved his hands into his pockets. He caught up with her easily, his shoes rapping against the stone streets. Up ahead, the dogs looked back but kept their easy pace.

"I came by to see you, and you were gone," she said in a soft voice. "Your friend Clive told me where to find you."

That damn Clive. He was probably the reason Nelson Biggers made Golden the Marseilles offer the same day Leonie rejected him. Forty-eight hours later, he'd been on a ship for France. Quick, and almost painless.

"I didn't think you'd be interested in knowing my forwarding address," he said. "Especially since I was just a piece of ass you were wasting time with for the summer."

"I never said those things!" Her raised voice ended on a cry. "I swear, I didn't."

"No, but your friends did, and you never told them they were wrong." His hands turned to fists in his pockets. "You never told me, either."

A wince tightened her face and she jerked her head away. "I was a coward," she said. "I never felt that about you, what my friends said."

"So, now what?" He didn't want to assume her presence meant anything more than her curiosity to see where he ended up. "You're here to apologize, to tell me how well school is going, what?"

"I missed you. I—I did what I should have done a long time ago and told my parents what I want." She turned away, her footsteps stuttering against the cobblestones, and made a growling sound of frustration. "This isn't going like I thought it would." Her shoulders hitched up to her ears, and her back became stiff and unyielding. She turned to him, her bottom lip caught between her teeth. "Can we— can we just start over? Please."

"Start over...so we can end up where?"

"At the place you said. Remember?"

She couldn't be talking about...that. Instead of assuming, he crossed his arms and waited.

"I messed up. I was stupid." Another bite into the plumpness of her lower lip. "I'm sorry." She held a letter clutched in her hand with a look of naked desperation on her face. "Golden, please." She sighed his name and the envelope in her hand crinkled loudly as she crushed it between the nervous flex of her fingers.

"Please what, Leonie?"

Sucker that he was, Golden was already halfway where he knew she wanted him to be. She'd crossed an *ocean* for him. With her at his side, the hole in his chest already felt a little smaller. His breath came easier.

But he needed to be sure this wasn't another game. "I'm listening."

"Please take me back." She stopped and grabbed his sleeve. "Take *us* back." She pressed her lips together and darted her gaze around them, at the narrow street with its faint glow of light, the sea undulating darkly beyond the harbor. "Will you have me, Golden, as stupid as I've been? Will you allow me to walk on this journey with you?"

"That's a foolish question, Leonie."

Her face crumbled and she jerked back, but he caught her around the waist and pulled her close. Her slight body trembled against his.

"I've been waiting for you to catch up to me for months."

A tentative smile lifted the corners of her trembling lips. She squeezed her eyes shut and leaned into him. "Oh, thank God," she whispered softly. The new lines on her face melted away. She smiled wider, revealing that unexpected dimple he'd always loved.

I love you. He didn't say the words that had been real for him for months now.

I love you, too. She didn't have to say what glowed in her dark eyes like a promise of forever.

"Would you like to go for a walk with me?" He gestured toward the street and the path leading to his apartment.

"Of course." Leonie clutched him tight, crinkling the letter against her stomach. The sound of it seemed to remind her she carried it. "I have something for you," she said. "For later." Her soft breath, smelling faintly of champagne, puffed against his throat. She pressed a kiss there.

A shudder rippled through him, a spark and a promise.

Yes, they would have a *later*. And a journey, and a life together. He offered her his arm and she took it, squeezed it with another of her dimpled smiles.

"You make me happy," she said, and the lights in her eyes told Golden this didn't surprise her anymore.

He chuckled, glad she finally realized it. "I know, lioness."

Their footsteps fell in sync on the cobblestoned street and they set off into the lamp-lit night. Together.

ON-AIR PASSION EXCERPT

"You should just keep your mouth shut! Nobody wants to hear politics from a ballplayer."

From behind the broad back of his bodyguard, Ahmed moved quickly through the vocal crowd of about two dozen people to get to the doors of the radio station. Some were obviously gawking simply because of who he was—rich, retired at thirty and a consistent presence in the Atlanta club scene and on gossip sites across the internet. Others were there because they smelled a scandal or something close to it. And there were some who were present, like the guy who'd just screamed at Ahmed, because they apparently didn't have anything better to do at ten o'clock on a Wednesday morning.

"Technically you're an *ex*-ballplayer, so you can have opinions on anything you damn well please." Sam, Ahmed's bodyguard and cousin, growled the comment as they slid past the radio station's security guys, just low enough for Ahmed to hear, although if he'd said it at the top of his voice, nobody would have reacted. Guys over six feet tall with muscles stacked on top of muscles could get away with saying just about anything they wanted to, and to whomever.

Ahmed was built on a more modest but—he liked to think—no

less impressive scale with his six and a half feet of lean but defined muscle, a strong jawline and cheekbones that had been accused a time or two of being "chiseled." And those were just the nice things his sisters said about him.

Only the memory of the mellow breakfast he'd had with his family—his sisters, Aisha and Devyn, his mother and Sam—kept his annoyance at the heckler to a low-grade ripple. Besides, the hostility of strangers was nothing new to him, especially after twelve years playing professional basketball. He was now retired and having fun being a part-time radio show host. Even if he'd been silent about his politics, people would still find some way to throw insults his way. Plenty of his former teammates were prime examples of that. The people loved you when you were playing well, making them money, entertaining them. But once you fumbled, good luck.

"Damn, they're rowdy out there today." Sam settled the lines of his dark jacket more firmly on his shoulders with a shrug, the custom-made suit easily hiding his gun and somehow minimizing the size, but not the threat, of his big body. Ahmed didn't know how he could wear it with the crazy-hot January weather currently punishing Atlanta. "What the hell did you do while I was asleep?" His deep voice rumbled in a way that let Ahmed know he was only half joking. Before going their separate ways—Sam to the military and Ahmed to basketball—Sam was forever pulling Ahmed out of the trouble his big mouth got him into. He'd learned to temper his snark-iness but once Sam got out of the army with an honorable discharge, Sam fell back into the role as bodyguard but in a more official capacity.

"You know it's because of that tweet I sent last night," Ahmed said.

"As if the city didn't already know how you felt about it closing that downtown high school." Sam took in the wide and sterile hallway and the half dozen or so people making their way through it with a skilled gaze, taking in details Ahmed took for granted.

"Just making sure they didn't miss my opinion," he said with a scornful twist of his lips.

Marcus Garvey High was a school Ahmed had poured a lot of money and time into to support its STEM program that worked to give city kids an equal chance at tech, engineering and science jobs once they graduated. Although Ahmed had been born into a middle-class family and hadn't faced the challenges many of those kids at the high school did, he knew betting on an elusive sports career or going into the armed forces shouldn't be the only options they saw in their future.

Ahmed was sick of urban kids' education being a low priority. Something had to be done about securing their future. He may not be a politician or even a "real activist," by some standards but he was doing what he could while he had the platform.

"Don't forget we're going to that town hall meeting on Monday morning," Ahmed said.

"Good," Sam said, nodding.

As they made their way toward the studio Ahmed would occupy for the next three hours, Sam walked just behind and to the right of Ahmed, keeping an eye out for whatever possible dangers lurked nearby. Not that Ahmed had stumbled into any hazards after being at the station for his new gig for nearly two months now. The weekly midmorning show was still enjoyable. It gave him a chance to interact with fans—and haters—in a personal way he'd never had the chance to try before. And it was something for him to do after retirement that didn't involve groupies, the successful string of restaurant franchises he'd bought or the various "investment people" he'd had to hire once his money began multiplying even faster than he'd planned.

Sam stepped ahead to push open the door of the studio, and Ahmed moved to step through it when a flash of pink caught his eye, something unusual in his established Wednesday-morning routine. He stopped in his tracks and damn near caught his breath at the vision of femininity floating toward him from down the hallway.

High heels, a pink floral dress swirling around slender legs and hips, a narrow waist he could easily measure with both of his hands. The woman's breasts were small, barely a handful, but like most

Black men he socialized with, Ahmed had never been caught up in breast size. Big, small, barely there at all—it didn't matter to him. The rear view was what made him decide whether or not a woman was worth a second look or even a second date.

The Pink Lady sauntered toward him, her hips swaying and high heels loudly kissing the tile floors, making his heart beat faster as she came close. She wore her hair straight and pinned up in some sort of topknot with curly wisps floating around her face.

"Don't swallow your tongue." Sam, still holding the door open, was making a visible effort not to roll his eyes.

Ahmed didn't care. He was already losing himself in a daydream involving thick thighs and a plump backside made for spanking. He had no idea what his Pink Lady was packing in her trunk, but *damn*, he bet it was good. His fingers twitched with the phantom sensation of sinking into her sweet flesh.

Sam pretended to cough into his fist. "Okay, now you're just being a creep."

And he was right. Ahmed couldn't stop himself from just...staring. He didn't want to stop. Above her hips and waist and delicate-looking breasts, the woman's face was *pretty*. Like a daisy in sunlight or a rainbow after a storm, she stunned him with her natural and easy radiance. The image came to him, effortlessly, of tumbling with her into his bed to the music of her laughter and the sweet clasp of her thighs while her thick hair fanned over his pillow.

Damn. She made him want to give up his rule about messing around at work.

But he wasn't a kid anymore. He couldn't afford to be that sloppy about who he took to his bed. Not again.

His—no—*the* Pink Lady was still walking toward Ahmed, but he forced himself to look away from her.

"Let's get in there and do this." He clapped his hands once, a loud gunshot of a noise to get his mind right.

"I'm not the one who needs the pep talk about sticking to business, cousin." Despite his casual words, Sam did his usual thorough scan of the studio's large outer office, only relaxing his stance once he was satisfied nothing lurked in the spacious room to harm Ahmed on his watch.

"Ahmed, my man!" The station's general manager, Clive Ramirez, was a ball of energy. Probably from the four-plus espressos he usually had before lunch.

He stepped out from behind the receptionist's desk, where he had been looking over the young woman's shoulder at something on her computer. With a wide grin, he shook Ahmed's hand. Firm and enthusiastic.

"What's going on, Clive?"

"Life, just life." Short yet muscular, with a belly just beginning to grow from middle age and lack of exercise, Clive Ramirez gave the impression of being a perennially happy man. He loved what he did for a living, fairly treated the people who worked for him, and loved drama like a teenage girl. But everyone had to have a hobby.

Clive followed Ahmed and Sam from the outer offices to the sound booth.

"Nothing wrong with that." Ahmed took off his blazer and draped it over one of the six chairs in the room while Sam stood with his back against the wall, his legs spread, hands clasped easily in front of him as he kept an eye on the single door into the room and the glass partition separating the sound booth from the studio, where the sound engineer and his intern handled their responsibilities.

Over the airwaves, Ahmed could hear DJ Don Juan, who was in the sound booth across the hall, about to wrap up his morning show.

"What's on tap for today?" Ahmed asked Clive. "Anything special or do I just do my thing?" His *thing* was usually to play music, rile up the listeners and entertain them with what his mother called his bee-sting humor. Ahmed would almost do this for free. He settled down into the ergonomic chair with a sigh of bone-deep pleasure then swiveled around to keep Clive in his sights.

The station's GM sat in the chair on the opposite side of the oblong table and its six microphones set up in the center of the soundproof room. "More of the usual," Clive said. "Except we have a Valentine's Day promotion going on. A local woman is supposed to come on with you today to plug her business." He passed Ahmed a sheet of paper. "It's all here. Just introduce her and her business then offer the prize. If it goes well, people will be calling in to win, and she'll get her money's worth in new clients."

"Cool, I can do that." He quickly scanned the paper, noting the type of business, the name of the owner and what she offered. He smirked before he could get his face under control. "Selling romance, huh?"

"What? You got something against selling love? `Tis the season, my friend."

Ahmed shrugged, not bothering to offer his opinion about romance or love in general. None of the so-called relationships he'd experienced had anything remotely like "love" attached to them. He didn't want to seem like the Grinch or whatever the Valentine's Day equivalent was.

"If you like it, I love it," he said and caught the flicker of amusement on Sam's otherwise stoic face.

Ahmed hid his hand behind his back and shot his cousin the bird. This time, Sam's amusement came with a huff of quiet laughter.

Minutes later, Ahmed eased into the seat, once DJ Don Juan wrapped up his program. He slipped on the headphones and into his on-air persona.

"Hey, Atlanta! It's Ahmed Clark on the air and in your ear for the next—" he looked at his watch, a gift from his father "—two hours and fifty-eight minutes. If you want to talk, call me. If you want to listen, open your ears real wide." And he was off. Grin in place, anticipation for the next few hours bubbling under his skin.

Yeah, he could definitely do this for free.

He fell into the magic of being on air, exchanging laughter and information with his listeners until he got the signal from the sound engineer's intern outside the glass. She flashed him five fingers. Almost time for Gabrielle Marshall to get on the microphone to hawk her goods. He gave Kiara the thumbs-up sign and started to wind down his heated discussion with a listener about citizen responsibility in the digital age. When the woman kept insisting regular people didn't need to share everything they recorded on their cell phones, especially when it came to footage that would inflame the public, Ahmed cut her off with Rihanna's "Desperado."

When Kiara gave him the thirty-second warning, he was ready. The door to the sound booth opened. And it turned out he wasn't prepared.

The Pink Lady from the hallway swept in on a cloud of crisp perfume, like she brought the spirit of autumn in with her, and Ahmed couldn't help but inhale a deep breath of it. The pen he'd been making a note with dropped from his numb fingers and rolled across the notebook, across the desk and then to the floor. He heard Sam snickering. A signal for him to get it together. For real.

But damn, she had dimples. They bracketed her quick smile, and she sank gracefully into the chair across from him to easily fit the headphones over her high swirl of neatly pinned hair. Three diamond studs in varying sizes winked from the lobe of one ear.

"Hi, I'm Gabrielle Marshall," she said. "Most people call me Elle."

Her voice was pure sex. And damn if she wasn't even sweeter looking up close. The smiling lips with just a hint of color. Big Bambi eyes and thick hair he could easily sink his hands into. He forced himself to pay attention to the now instead of the hypothetical future where he had her in his bed. He held out his hand for her to shake.

"Ahmed."

She smiled wider, a curve of glistening and lusciously full lips that made him glad he was sitting down. After releasing her soft hand, he reached under the desk to subtly adjust himself.

Although Sam didn't make another sound, Ahmed could feel his amusement from all the way across the room.

Ahmed cleared his throat and glanced at the timer. "I'll introduce you after this song. You already know what to do, right?"

Why did that sound dirty?

The Pink Lady—Elle—nodded and settled her little purse on the desk. Her lips curved again. The pulse of heat in Ahmed's slacks made him wince. A woman's smile. Really? That was what was getting him hard these days? He must really need to get laid. He could easily picture her being the next woman sprawled, wet and panting, in his bed.

"Here we go," he croaked.

<u>Available Now.</u>

THANK YOU!

Thank you so much for reading A DELICATE AFFAIR! If you enjoyed it, please take the time to **write a starred review** online – it doesn't have to be a long one – and share your experience with a friend or three.

To keep up with the latest releases and get free reads, subscribe to my newsletter here: http://bit.ly/2mmWggl.

To find me on the web, go to my website www.LindsayEvansWrites.com, Facebook, Twitter, or Tumblr pages. You can even contact me by email: LindsayEvansXOX@gmail.com.

DECADES: A JOURNEY OF AFRICAN AMERICAN ROMANCE

Continue the journey with these compelling, unforgettable stories:

* January 2018: A Delicate Affair by Lindsay Evans (1900s), LindsayEvansWrites.com

* February 2018: A Secret Desire by Kaia Danielle (1910s), https://about.me/kaiawrites

* March 2018: Love's Serenade by Sheryl Lister (1920s), SherylLister.com

* April 2018: The Art of Love by Suzette Harrison (1930s), SDHBooks.com

* May 2018: Love's Sweet Melody by Kianna Alexander (1940s), AuthorKiannaAlexander.com

* June 2018: Pride and Passion by Carla Buchanan (1950s), CarlaBuchanan.com

* July 2018: Promise Me a Dream by Wayne Jordan (1960s), WayneJordan.net

* August 2018: Election Day by Keith Thomas Walker (1970s), KeithWalkerBooks.com

* September 2018: Made to Hold You by Elle Wright (1980s), ElleWright.com

* October 2018: Thug Love by Zuri Day (1990s), ZuriDay.com

* November 2018: Inconsequential Circumstances by Denise Jeffries (2000s), DeniseJeffries.com

* December 2018: Campaign for Her Heart by Patricia Sargeant (2010s), PatriciaSargeant.com

ALSO BY LINDSAY EVANS

Novels Available Now

Affair of Pleasure

Bare Pleasures (Miami Strong)

The CEO's Dilemma

On-Air Passion (The Clarks of Atlanta)

Pleasure Under the Sun

Snowy Mountain Nights

Sultry Pleasure: A Billionaire Romance

The Pleasure of His Company (Miami Strong)

Untamed Love

The Wrong Fiancé

Professional Lovers Series

Seducing the Stripper (Professional Lovers Series Book 1)

Novella Anthology

Dim the Lights

ABOUT THE AUTHOR

Born in Jamaica, Lindsay Evans currently lives and writes in Madrid, Spain. A writer of sensual love stories, she loves good food and romance and would happily travel to the ends of the earth for both. Find out more at www.LindsayEvansWrites.com.